Hamburger, Holy Cow!

Lois Fletcher
Illustrated by Wil Foster

Wesleyan Publishing House
Indianapolis, Indiana

Table of Contents

"Namaste!" 7

Chicken Coops and Goose Bumps 17

Going Through the Hoops 29

Holy Cow! 45

Working Hands, Praying Hands 59

A Great Adventure 69

Indian Merchant 79

The Essay 89

Changing Attitudes 99

Zone Out 107

Letters Home 121

Home Cooking 133

The Boy in the Mirror 147

"Alvida" 159

"Namaste!"

R aja stiffened as the plane descended and the wheels made contact with the tarmac at New York's La Guardia Airport. Through the small oval window, the ground lights were a brilliant, flashing blur as the plane roared down the runway. It was night in America. The plane taxied to the terminal and Raja gradually relaxed. Still, he felt as if he had butterflies in his stomach. It had been a very long trip and India seemed so far away. With trembling legs, he walked slowly down the ramp into the waiting area. He anxiously searched the crowd for his host family. They had sent him a photograph, but would he recognize them in this crowd? Maybe he should have sent one of himself. What if they had changed their minds and decided not to come? What would happen to him?

Just then he saw his name on a sign held high above the crowd. This must be my host family, he thought, approaching nervously. Yes, of course, those two had to be Mr. and Mrs. Jade. They looked exactly like the picture. And the boy with them would be Brad. His hair was a little different and he was taller than in the picture, but that was surely Brad Jade. He was taller than Raja, but one year younger. Brad was sixteen and a grade lower, Raja had been told. Raja tried to remember how the Americans termed it. He would be a senior and Brad would be a junior. Yes, that was it.

And there, the one energetically waving the sign back and forth, that could only be Mitsuko, the fifteen-year-old adopted Japanese daughter. She would be a sophomore.

"Over here, Raja!" she called, waving the sign and smiling warmly. "Namaste!" she cried out, which was the Hindi word for "hello." A bright spot in this strange land, her smile immediately made him feel welcome. At the same time, something about her reminded him of his own two sisters, Devika and Runa, so far away in India. He felt a sudden, sharp pang of homesickness as he realized it would be next June before he would see them again—nine months before they would smile up at him as Mitsuko was smiling now.

But it was Mitsuko's smile that warmed him, helping to push back the momentary sadness he felt. He smiled back, extended his hand in greeting, and approached his host family. After shaking hands and introducing themselves to Raja, the Jades led him through the busy airport, located his luggage, and helped him carry the suitcases and bags to their car. Sandwiched between Mitsuko and Brad in the back seat of the car, Raja craned his neck, trying to see everything he could as they drove out of the parking garage. Even though it was night, there was so much to see in the glare of the big spotlights. Mr. Jade drove carefully around the winding exit ramp of the parking garage and through the tollgate.

He then began to accelerate as he took the on-ramp to the expressway. Raja's eyes widened in apprehension as Mr. Jade skillfully maneuvered through the rush of vehicles whizzing by them on the right and left.

"So many cars, I have never seen!" Raja exclaimed, turning in his seat and watching the approaching headlights of the traffic behind them. "And so many lanes! The people, where do they walk?" he asked.

"Not on this highway, if they value their lives," Mitsuko quipped. "In the cities and towns, there are sidewalks along the roads for them to walk on. You will see soon enough."

Even in the dark interior of the car, speeding along an American highway at night, Raja was able to see many new things—huge buildings with hundreds of windows and thousands of lights shining through them, big billboards with colorful pictures, busy restaurants and gas stations. When they turned off the main highway and began to drive along a two-way road, the tall buildings were gradually replaced with smaller buildings and clusters of houses. Although many of the buildings were dark, most of the houses were brightly lit. Raja could see through some of the windows into people's homes. In one, he saw a television screen flickering. In another house, a family was sitting around a table. Brad nudged Raja gently and told him they were almost home. Fighting back another wave of homesickness, Raja turned and watched Mitsuko as she chattered. She was pointing out a cat sitting in a windowsill. She did not speak with an accent like he did and he wondered how long she had lived in America. She grinned at him and he smiled back. She certainly did bounce and move her hands a lot when she was talking! He wondered whether every American girl did that.

They turned into the driveway of a two-story brick home. "We're here, Raja," Brad announced. "This is your new home."

Raja was startled when the garage door opened all by itself and Mr. Jade drove in.

"How that happen, the door opening for you, Mr. Jade?" Raja asked, a little self-conscious about his speech.

"That, Raja, is all because of this little wonder called a remote control. See, we push this button and the garage door goes up or down," Mr. Jade replied. He handed the remote control to Raja, who pushed the button and laughed as the garage door rolled down.

As they got out of the car and carried Raja's luggage into the kitchen, Raja couldn't hide his amazement.

"What a beautiful home you are having, Mr. and Mrs. Jade!" Raja exclaimed. "And so big!"

Mrs. Jade smiled at him. "Raja, if you like, you may call us Mom and Dad while you live with us. We are very happy to have you as our son for this year." She turned to Mitsuko and Brad. "Mitsuko, why don't you show Raja around and then help him carry his things to his room? Brad, would you take the heavier suitcases upstairs for them, please?"

Mitsuko took Raja on a quick tour of the downstairs. He couldn't believe how many rooms there were.

There was one called a family room that had a sofa and TV, and a room with another sofa called the living room. He didn't quite understand why there were two rooms with two sofas. The dining room was very nice, but he wondered why it was needed, since there was also a table and chairs in the kitchen. Did the Americans have two of everything? And oddest of all, there was even a room for washing the clothes!

"I'll show you around outside tomorrow when it's light," Mitsuko said, hoisting one of his bags over her shoulder. They climbed the stairs and she rattled off who belonged in each bedroom, as if she were a tour guide. Then she opened a door halfway down the hall.

"This is your room, Raja," she said, stepping inside and turning on the light. "And right next to it is your bathroom. You can put some of your things in these dresser drawers and also hang clothes in this closet. I hope you like it." She seemed quiet. She wasn't bouncing and moving her hands around, almost as if she realized he was trying to take in everything. "Hey, Raja, why don't you take a few minutes to settle in, then come down and join us for a bedtime snack?" She closed the door behind her.

Raja put the satchel he was holding on the bed and sat down. The room was so big! Was this his own bathroom? There was even a desk just for him where he could study his school lessons and write letters to his friends and family back home.

Suddenly he realized how very alone he was. Mother and Devika weren't here to unpack for him. In

America he would have to learn to take care of his own clothes.

Each thing he unpacked and placed in dresser drawers or hung in the closet reminded him of home and family. Here was the new shirt Mother had bought him. He folded it carefully, just as Devika had shown him. Here was the book his little sister, Runa, had given him to read. He set it on the nightstand along with two Bibles, one Hindi and the other English. At home he read the Hindi Bible every morning when he got up and the English Bible every night before he went to bed. He would continue to do that here in America, just as his father had taught him.

After unpacking, he opened the door and nervously peered out. It was quiet upstairs but he could hear the sound of cheerful conversation below. He followed the sound into the kitchen, where the Jades were seated at the kitchen table. Brad motioned him to join them, patting the empty chair next to him. Raja recognized the glass of milk, but wasn't so sure about the sandwich on the plate. He took a sip of milk. How strange this tasted! Not at all like the milk in India, which had to be boiled first. He smiled politely and managed to drink it without thinking too much about the taste. As for the sandwich, now that was different. He carefully peeled back the bread and examined the meat.

"I am being sorry, Mrs.—, ah, Mom, but raw meat I cannot be eating," he said, hoping he was not offending her.

Mrs. Jade chuckled. "That's all right, Raja. You will

learn to eat some new things in America. Actually, this is not raw meat at all. This is a kind of lunchmeat we call bologna. You may learn to like it later. Perhaps you would like some cookies instead?"

"Thank you, but I am thinking the trip was long and I am very tired and I will to bed be going."

Raja was thankful for the privacy of his room. He did not realize just how tired he was until he slipped off his shoes and felt his toes sink down into the soft, thick, bedroom carpet. How good that felt! He locked his bedroom door and then opened the curtains of the window. There were no bars on the windows! Would he be safe? He checked the lock on the window and then closed the curtains.

After such a long trip, Raja felt grimy and decided to shower before going to bed. How white and shiny everything looked in this bathroom! And how strange the stool looked so high off the floor. Everything in America was strange. Even the shower was different. It had a tub under it and a curtain all around. At home his family's shower was very narrow and had one faucet. This American one had three faucets. What could they all be for? He stepped into the tub and slowly turned a faucet. Hot water? They have hot water? Ouch, too hot! Stepping back a little, he turned another faucet. Aha. This was the cold water. He experimented with both faucets until the water was the right temperature, but wondered why it still did not come out of the showerhead. When he jiggled the third handle, he received his answer. The first rush of water was cool and he jumped. But it quickly warmed and he sighed gratefully. Warm water! This was exactly what he needed! And practical, too, since he had noticed already how much cooler the weather was here than in India. It would definitely be too cool for a cold shower in this part of America! He bent his head under the warm flow of water and felt all his anxiety and exhaustion rinse away.

Before going to bed, he turned on the nightstand light and turned off the bedroom light. Peeking out the window, he saw that the neighborhood was quiet. More and more of the houses were dark, as people prepared for sleep. In the distance, the lights of the unfamiliar city reminded him that he was far from home. Overhead, however, the familiar pattern of stars reminded him that God was still watching over him, whether he was in India or America.

Raja reached for his English Bible and read a few verses.

Raja reached for his English Bible and read a few verses. Then he knelt beside his bed and thanked God for bringing him safely to America. He also asked God to care for his family while he was so far away.

There was one more puzzle to solve. Raja stood looking at the bed with the beautiful cover, and wondered how to get in. He peeled back the bedspread, like he had peeled back the bread on the bologna sandwich. Was he supposed to sleep on top of these sheets or under them? He would have to ask Mom tomorrow. For now, he would play it safe. Yawning, he slipped under the bedspread and settled on top of the sheets. His mind turned over the events of the day, then gradually drifted to thoughts of his home in India. It would be morning there. Mother would be riding the rickshaw to the junior college where she taught. Father would be riding his motorcycle to the college where he was a professor. Both Devika and Runa would be on their way to school. He missed them so much.

As sleep moved in to claim him, he thought, I will prove to my family that I can take care of myself. This year away from home will teach me responsibility, so that someday I will be able to care for my parents in their old age. I'll make them proud of me!

Chicken Coops and Goose Bumps

Raja shivered in his sleep. Instinctively, he tugged the bedspread up under his chin. Something wasn't quite right. Blinking drowsily, he opened his eyes—and was suddenly, completely awake. Even in a room darkened by closed curtains, he could see enough to know that he was not in India. He sat straight up in bed and tried to order his thoughts. He remembered that he had traveled over 50 hours by train and plane and was now in America. He remembered Brad and Mitsuko, the long drive from the airport, pushing the button on the remote control, a piece of slick, shiny meat called bologna. The images tumbled around in his mind.

With something close to panic, he glanced at the bedside clock. Oh no! It was nearly noon! He'd slept over 12 hours! What would his host family think?

He scrambled out of bed and hastily straightened the covers. He had to remember to ask Mrs. Jade if he was to sleep under the sheets or on top of them. Wait, he had to remember to call her Mom. She seemed to like that.

Worried about being late, he decided not to shower, especially since he had showered last night. But there was one thing he would not forget to do, no matter how late it was. Raja sat on the edge of the bed and reached for his Hindi Bible and began to read where he had last left off. Despite his best efforts to concentrate on what he was reading, he couldn't help but think of his own family in India. If it were noon here, it would be 9:30 p.m. there. His mother, father, and two sisters would be getting ready for bed. How he wished his sisters were here for him to tease. The three of them had such fun before his parents would settle them down for family devotions each night. Smiling at the memory, it suddenly hit him that they would probably be kneeling in prayer at this very moment.

Although time and distance separated them, Raja immediately knelt beside his bed and began to pray. His parents' strong faith had always been an example to him. He remembered his mother's smooth, lovely hands folded in prayer, his father's head bent humbly. Raja spoke to God as he always had from childhood— in simple words, talking to God as if He were right there in the room with him. As he prayed, he felt at peace with God and close to his family, even though they were miles away.

He arose and dressed, now properly prepared to begin his new life in America.

Mitsuko greeted him with another bright smile as he entered the kitchen. He remembered her cheerful smile under the waving sign at the airport last night, her bouncy manner of walking, and the way her hands gestured when she was talking. He was glad he had not been dreaming and that Mitsuko was the same now as she had been last night.

"Mother and Father are off to work and Brad has gone to soccer practice," she said. "So you're stuck with me. What would you like for breakfast? I'll give you a hint, Raja. I've already made French toast." She grinned mischievously, as if daring him to ask for something else.

"French toast is good. In India we have that too," he answered politely. He was aware that his English was choppy and singsong. He knew that he said the "w" sound like a "v and the "th" sound like a "d." Still, Mitsuko did not seem to mind.

She heated up the French toast and divided it between two plates, then sat down at the table with him. Before they ate, she led them in a simple prayer, thanking God for the food before them and asking Him to provide for those in the world who did not have enough food. She also thanked Him for bringing Raja to them safely.

Raja watched as she spread butter on her pieces of French toast and then poured syrup over them. She passed the butter and syrup to him and he did just as she had done.

This was like home where his sisters waited on him, he thought, tasting the syrup and finding it to be sweet and delicious. But he wondered if Mitsuko would let him tease her as he did his sisters. Perhaps in time he could? For now he was content to watch her cut the French toast.

"Some people sprinkle theirs with confectioner's sugar, you know," she was mumbling as she chewed. "Or regular sugar with cinnamon. How do you like it, Raja?"

"This is the best I am ever having," he declared, stabbing a triangle of bread with his fork.

Her friendly chatter continued while he ate. He didn't realize how hungry he was! There was still the matter of the milk, however. He forced himself to drink it without revealing on his face that it was going to take some time to adjust to such a strange flavor!

When they had finished eating, Mitsuko said, "OK, now for the fun part, Raja. The dishes!" She made a funny face and beckoned him to join her at the sink. "Lucky us, huh? Everybody else just flew the coop and left us the mess. Do you want to wash or dry?"

Raja hesitated a moment before picking up a dishtowel. He had to do dishes? But this was servant's work! What would his grandmother think if she could see him now—with a dishtowel in his hands? And what did Mitsuko mean by "flew the coop"? Did they have chickens here?

Mitsuko didn't seem to notice Raja's bewildered face. She hummed as she rinsed the dishes under the hot water faucet and then put them in a sink full of hot, soapy water to be washed. Then she rinsed them again and put them in the rack for Raja to dry.

"When you finish drying them, you can stack them

on the counter and we will both put them away. That way, you'll learn where things go, OK?"

"OK," he answered, gingerly picking up a dish as if it might bite him. He flashed a broad, nervous smile at Mitsuko and began to rub the dish. He should have paid more attention to how his sisters did such work. He suspected that this was the first of many cultural adjustments he would have to make in America.

"Raja," Mitsuko was saying, trying hard not to laugh, "you're going to rub the design off that dish. Why don't you put that one down and try another one?"

Raja's face flushed and his embarrassed smile broadened, displaying his perfect teeth—brilliantly white against his dark skin.

"Mother would not be letting me touch her dishes," he said. "She would be afraid of me dropping them!"

Mitsuko laughed. "You're doing fine, Raja. What was your kitchen like at home?"

"Much different here from India," he began. "We have a sink in our house, but it is not like that in many places. Often the villages are having only one pump or faucet where the people take their dishes for washing them in cold water."

Mitsuko listened carefully while they worked, asking questions every so often. Raja was pleased that she was so interested in what he had to say and that she did not correct his English. When at last they were done and the dishes were put away, Mitsuko asked if Raja wanted her to show him around the neighborhood.

Raja answered eagerly, "Yes, that would be good!"

He was anxious to see what he had not been able to see on the drive home last night. He was more rested and alert now, too. Following Mitsuko out the door, he stopped suddenly.

"Mitsuko!" he cried in alarm, rubbing his right hand over his left arm. "These little bumps! What they are? A disease I am catching?"

Mitsuko's bell-like laughter echoed around him. "No, silly," she teased. "Those are goose bumps!" She ran inside and came back out with his jacket.

At his look of confusion, she stopped smiling. Her jaw dropped open. "You've never had goose bumps, Raja? Wow, India must be really, really hot. It's not even winter here yet!" She draped his jacket around his shoulders, standing on her toes to reach up and help him. She then tugged on his arm to get him to follow her down the sidewalk.

"C'mon, Raja," she encouraged. "You'll warm up once we get going. Goose bumps are nature's way of helping your body adjust to changes in temperature. They'll go away in a few minutes. In time, you'll get used to the cooler weather. You'll see."

Raja gave Mitsuko another one of his broad, nervous grins. Perhaps she was teasing him? First she was talking about chicken coops and now she was telling him about goose bumps. It was very strange the way Americans talked about poultry. And he hadn't seen a chicken or a goose anywhere!

Still, the fresh afternoon air smelled wonderful. India was always dusty and dry. As he walked alongside

Mitsuko, he turned his head from side to side, trying to see everything at once. He noticed that all the houses had big areas of grass around them. Although it was very pretty to look at, it seemed wasteful to him. He asked Mitsuko about that.

"We call the grass around each house a lawn, Raja," she explained. "It is something Americans like, although they complain about mowing the grass. For that, we use a lawnmower. Lawns are nice for children to play in, or for grownups to sit on. Sometimes we eat outside on our lawn, like we're having a picnic. Mostly, I think we like them because they give us some space between houses."

"Our houses in India are very close together and there is no room for lawns," Raja replied. "That would be wasting space for the houses we are needing for the many peoples who are not having a home." Raja was sure his words were all mixed up and he hoped Mitsuko would understand what he was trying to say.

Mitsuko nodded thoughtfully and Raja relaxed. He appreciated the way she listened to what he was saying instead of the way he said it. It was easy to talk to her.

"The lawns are nice, Mitsuko," he added. He did not want to make her uncomfortable about the differences in the way they lived. "I am liking them. Maybe if we were having lawns in my country, it would not be so dusty."

They were now walking alongside a busy street. There was much traffic, although not as much as he remembered on the highway last night. The cars were moving faster than the ones in India, but he was surprised that they traveled in such an orderly fashion. For the most part they stayed in lanes, following one another and stopping when the car ahead stopped. And there were no rickshaws or motorbikes or wagons or bicycles weaving around the cars. No cows ran loose on the sidewalks and in the streets! The people who were walking stayed on a side-way. No, that was not it. What had Mitsuko called it last night? Sidewalk? Yes, sidewalk. And that is what the people were doing: walking on the side of the road. How very curious!

He was so lost in thought as he tried to process everything he was seeing and hearing, that he didn't notice when Mitsuko stopped at the corner. He heard the screech of brakes and Mitsuko's scream as she rushed forward and pulled him back onto the sidewalk.

When he realized he had stepped in front of a car, Raja's heart began to pound.

"I am sorry, Mitsuko. What was I doing wrong?" he asked, suddenly finding it hard to talk.

"You're OK, Raja. Just relax a minute," she said. He could tell she was having a little trouble relaxing herself. "Looks like I'm going to need a leash for you!" she quipped. That made him smile a little. "Now, Raja, it's very important for you to pay attention at all times when you're around traffic. You have traffic lights in India, don't you?"

"The red and green lights? In some places we have them. Mostly no one is paying them any attention," he answered.

"Well, Raja, you HAVE to pay attention to them here, do you understand?" she said. There was no kidding tone

"I am sorry, Mitsuko. What was I doing wrong?"

in her voice. "Do not ever cross a street unless it is safe to do so. See the light there? When it is green facing you, you can cross the street. When it is red, you must wait. These lights here have a small sign underneath that tell you to walk or not to walk. Sometimes you will see lights that have a hand in the red part, and a picture of a person walking in the green part."

He nodded to let her know he was listening carefully.

"Even so, Raja," she continued, locking eyes with him, "you must always look before you cross. Even if the light is green, you must look both ways and behind you to make sure a car is not running a red light, or forgetting to give you the right of way. Remember, you must never argue with a car."

"They are being bigger than I am," he said solemnly.

"You've got that right!" Mitsuko exclaimed, finally

breaking into her famous smile.

They crossed the street and continued their walk.

"In my country, the streets are very different with very many peoples all mixed together and riding very many different things. We are having many more bicycles and they are in the street with the cars and trucks. Where are your cows?"

"Cows?" Mitsuko asked, her eyes twinkling. "Oh, I forgot about that. Raja, here in America our cows are out in the country on farms and ranches. They do not run free in the city."

He thought about that for a few seconds. "They are everywhere in India. Sometimes they decide to take a nap in the middle of the street and everyone is having to go around them."

Mitsuko laughed at that. He loved to hear her laugh. He continued, thinking she might enjoy hearing more about traffic in India. "But trucks are being the worst. They are weaving even more than the bicycles and cars, and squeezing in wherever there is a place. When a truck driver is seeing an opening, he blinks his lights to let others know that he is taking the opening and everyone is better to be getting out of the way. If a truck is breaking, the driver will leave it. It can sit in the middle of the street for many days."

"Taking a nap with the cows, huh?" Mitsuko joked.

He laughed and the laughter felt good inside. He was glad to be in America this afternoon, enjoying the afternoon sunshine and the many interesting sights and sounds and smells of this country. Realizing that he was no longer cold, he pulled his jacket from around his shoulders and draped it over his arm.

"Thank you, Mitsuko, for saving me from being hit by that car," he said softly. She said nothing. She smiled up at him, then linked her arm in his as they continued to walk around the neighborhood.

Returning home, Raja spotted a flower garden nearby and wandered over to examine it. Although his family's house in India did not have a lawn, his mother had a flower bed along the side of the house. She spent many hours working in it and the family had always enjoyed the beautiful flowers she cut for bouquets. Bending over to smell a dark red rose, he was suddenly overcome by the memory of her lovely hands arranging flowers in a vase, of the scent she carried on her clothing when she came in from working in her flower bed.

He kept that memory in his heart as he knelt by his bedside later that night. "Thank you, dear God, for protecting us today in the traffic. And please help me adjust to this new culture," he prayed. He remembered to climb under the sheets, as Mom had told him to. And he was grateful for the extra blanket she had given him. His first day in America had been a day full of many new experiences.

In his dreams that night, he dried dishes on the lawn while Mitsuko smiled at him from a chicken coop. A cow with goose bumps wandered up and fell asleep on the front step. And the roses in the flower bed were flashing red and green.

Going Through the Hoops

The early morning sunshine was warm on Raja's face as he awoke. He'd forgotten to close the bedroom curtains last night. Funny, it didn't seem to matter anymore that there weren't bars on the window. He hadn't even locked his bedroom door. He felt safe here. Yawning as he stretched and climbed out of bed, he realized that he also felt very rested on this beautiful September morning in America. It was Sunday morning, too. Today, he would attend church with his host family.

Quickly, he showered and dressed. He chose the suit his father had given him, one made in India especially for Raja to wear for such occasions. Checking himself carefully in the mirror, he selected a tie that complemented his suit, then brushed his curly black hair. He wanted to look his best when he walked into church with the Jade family. He had heard that being a Christian in America was something very normal, almost commonplace. Even as he walked with

Mitsuko yesterday, he noticed church steeples poking up throughout the town and beyond. In India, he and his family were in the minority and were sometimes ridiculed for their faith. Yes, it would be quite exciting to experience American Christianity. But even as excited as he was, Raja did not forget to read from his Hindi Bible and then kneel beside his bed to ask God's blessing on the day ahead.

"Wow, don't you look sharp!" exclaimed Mitsuko, as Raja stepped into the kitchen to join the family for breakfast. "I want to sit by you in church."

He flushed bright red but managed to smile and say, "Good morning, everyone." Accepting a plate from Mrs. Jade, he sat down at the table. The family had already said grace, so he bowed his head and prayed silently. He kept one eye open, though, as he studied the plate and tried to figure out just what it was he was thanking God for. It was a blob of bright yellow, speckled with green and red and pieces of something clear and shiny. Triangles of bread framed the plate, not cooked like French toast, but crisp and brown. Of course, there was the ever-present glass of milk, once again challenging him to flex his taste buds to the limits. He raised his head from prayer. Well, it was just best to get it over with, he decided, raising his fork like a weapon and preparing to attack.

As if reading his mind, Mrs. Jade said, "That's an omelet, Raja. Three eggs cooked with onions, red and green peppers, some shredded zucchini and cheese, then folded over. I buttered your toast, but you can put jelly on it, if you like."

Raja nodded politely, held his breath, and dug in. Everybody else must have been holding their breaths, too, because there was an audible sigh of relief when he chewed for a few moments, swallowed, raised his eyebrows and smiled. "This is very, very good, Mom," Raja said, meaning it.

Everyone relaxed and continued eating. "Are girls and boys and men and women sitting together in your church?" Raja asked Mr. Jade. "In India, the men sit on one side and the women are sitting on the other side of the church."

Mr. Jade replied, smiling kindly, "In most American churches, men and women sit together. A few churches, however, follow the tradition you have described. We just happen to attend a church where we like to sit together as a family. And we are very happy to have you as part of our family, Raja."

"Thanks," Raja said, relieved. "I was wondering where I would be sitting. It is good having family with you when you are being new to a place." It was also good, he decided, to get the milk out of the way, then finish eating. The delicious flavors of the omelet successfully covered the strong, unpleasant flavor of American milk.

Raja was aware of people staring at him as they walked from the church parking lot to the front entrance of the church. Brad hooked a brotherly arm around his shoulder, casually waving and calling out to his friends as he guided Raja along the sidewalk. Mitsuko walked protectively on his other side. At the entrance, Mr. Jade introduced Raja to the pastor and briefly explained the circumstances of his stay with them.

The pastor shook Raja's hand and smiled warmly. "Welcome to our church, Raja. It is wonderful to have you here with us today. I hope you will want to join us each Sunday."

The stares seemed to intensify as he walked down the aisle with his host family. Some people turned around in their pews to watch him. Once the Jade family was seated, Raja leaned close to Mitsuko and whispered, "I am the only one with dark skin in this church. Will I be looking down on, I mean, being looked down on because of my color?"

Mitsuko looked at Raja with a sad, sweet smile. "Raja," she whispered, "it is a terrible thing to admit, but, yes, there are people in America who will look down on you because of your color. Some look down on me because I am Japanese, even though I have lived here for many years and talk just like them. In India, I understand some of your people do the same to those with darker skin than yours."

Raja nodded and she continued. "So, there are some people, even in this church, who will not see past the color of your skin. But you are part of our family this year and most people will accept you without any question, so don't worry about being a different color, OK?"

"OK," he said. Raja was comforted that his host family was next to him and would support him. He was happy to be sitting between Brad and Mitsuko in the pew. As he glanced around, he noticed that other families were also sitting together. This was so different from India where the churches had long benches and he and the other young men would crowd together on one bench. The more they could get on one bench, the better it was. Even when the bench seemed to be full, latecomers could always find a spot. Raja watched as other families came up the aisle.

"Are we needing to move over and making room for them?" he asked Brad.

"No, it's OK, Raja," Brad said, checking on either side of them. "This pew is pretty full. There are plenty of other pews for them to sit in."

Pretty full? It did not seem that way to Raja at all! It seemed they could get lots more people into this pew. He thought about what Mitsuko had said about lawns around American houses. This must be something like that. Americans must like to have space around them all the time, he concluded. Even in church.

Someone announced the call to worship and the service began. Raja was surprised that the doors to the sanctuary closed behind them. In India, people straggled in all through the first half of the service. Being on time meant very little to them.

As the congregation began to sing the first hymn, Raja found the page in the hymnal and tried to follow the words. When he couldn't keep up, he whispered to Mitsuko, "Why are they so fast singing?"

"It just seems that way, Raja," she whispered back.

"You are not used to the pronunciation yet. You will soon learn to sing along with the rest of us. Do you recognize this hymn?"

"Yes, I do."

"Then sing along with us in your own language," she prompted. "The melody is the same."

He tried that and smiled as he found he was able to follow along. Nobody seemed to notice, either, so he sang with all his heart. Mitsuko had to tug on his sleeve to get him to sit down when the hymn concluded. He was ready to launch into another verse.

The pastor was making some announcements and Raja's thoughts drifted as he glanced around the sanctuary. Then Mitsuko was elbowing him again. He realized that the pastor had just announced his name and was talking about him.

"...who is living with the Jade family this coming school year," the pastor continued. "Raja is an exchange student from India and a fellow Christian. Please make him feel welcome when you leave today."

Raja was glad when the music began again and the people turned back to their hymnals. He'd had quite enough of being stared at!

During the sermon, Raja had trouble understanding everything the pastor said. When the pastor asked for prayer requests, Raja missed much of what the people were saying. Everyone talked so fast!

Although he didn't understand all of the message or the hymns, he could feel God's Spirit moving in the service. He understood enough to know that these people in America worshiped the same God as his family in India did.

After church, several families came up to him. Many of these people seemed genuinely pleased to meet him. They shook his hand and offered to help him any way they could.

On the way home, Mitusko asked, "What did you think, Raja?"

He was thoughtful and quiet for a moment before answering. "It was nice sitting with my American family, even when I am missing my friends all crowded on the bench. I am feeling welcome and shut out at the same time and the people are talking so fast is making me hard to understand them. Do they always be speaking so fast?" Mitsuko chuckled. "Give yourself time, Raja. Yesterday when you were talking Hindi to me, it seemed as if you were talking really fast, too. Things will get better. You'll see."

Raja settled back in the car seat between Brad and Mitsuko. He knew Mitsuko was right. He would just need time to adjust. Then his thoughts turned to what awaited him at the Jade home. He knew that Mrs. Jade had prepared a big Sunday dinner, one that they would eat in the big dining room and not at the kitchen table. He had helped Mitsuko last night set the table with the "good" silverware and another set of dishes called china. Ah, these Americans with two of everything! And eating a big meal in the middle of the day? Another cultural adjustment he would have to make. In India his family almost always ate their main meal at 8 o'clock each evening. At this point, however, Raja was not so much concerned about WHEN he would be eating as WHAT he would be eating. There had been some very strange smells indeed coming from that oven.

The next morning, Raja had barely finished his prayers when he heard Mitsuko calling to him.

"Wake up, Raja, you sleepyhead!" she hollered, hammering on his door. "We need to be on our way. Your appointment is at 9:30. You still have time for some cereal or toast if you hurry."

"I am coming," he said, rising quickly from his knees. Glancing at himself in the mirror one last time, making sure his uniform was not wrinkled and his hair was neatly brushed, he slung his backpack over one shoulder and hurried into the kitchen. He'd already decided against cereal. It wasn't the cereal so much as the American milk the cereal would be floating in. He opted for toast instead and dropped two slices of bread into the toaster. He wondered why Mitsuko was giving him such a curious look.

"Uh, Raja," she began somewhat hesitantly. "It's only registration. You don't have to dress up."

He set a plate on the counter and found a knife in the drawer. "I am not dressing up, Mitsuko," he said, holding his arms out to his sides and looking down at himself. "This is just my school uniform. All of us in India are wearing uniforms to school." As he buttered his toast, he thought Mitsuko looked especially pretty this morning. Her shoulder-length hair was straight and black, framing a round, pixie face and setting off her dark, almond-shaped eyes. Those eyes seemed to be dancing with amusement, however.

Taking a bite of his toast, he at last noticed that she was wearing jeans.

"Mitsuko," he said around a mouthful of toast, "you will be needing to hurry, but I will wait for you."

Her dark eyes looked amused as she arched her eyebrow. "Excuse me?" she remarked. "Why do you need to wait for me? I'm the one who's ready, Raja."

He looked puzzled. "But you are wearing jeans. Where your uniform is?"

Mitsuko laughed. "We don't wear uniforms. Most of us wear jeans to school."

Raja's look went from puzzled to shocked. He nearly choked on his toast. "I am being sorry, Mitsuko. In India girls do not be wearing jeans at all, especially not in school. This is most strange." He looked down again at his carefully creased blue pants, white shirt and red tie. Even though his sisters always did his ironing for him in India, he had ironed his own things last night.

Mitsuko was watching him with an odd little smile. Her hands were on her hips, as if she was waiting for something.

"I am sorry, Mitsuko," he said. "I am not meaning what I am saying, I mean, I should not say that. It is different in America. I understand this. Will you forgive me?"

"It's OK, Raja," she said with a smile. "No offense taken. Can you finish eating that while we walk?"

After grabbing his jacket from the coat rack on the

kitchen wall, he followed her out the door. "Will I be out of place in my uniform, Mitsuko?"

"You will be all right for registration, but you may want to dress more casually tomorrow. It's up to you, Raja."

Mitsuko had pointed out the high school on their Saturday walk. He was glad that it was only four blocks from home. He had heard that many American students rode buses and sometimes had to travel long distances to their schools. As they approached the front entrance to the school, Mitsuko waved to a girl with long yellow hair.

"Sierra, come here and meet my friend, Raja. He is an exchange student from India who is living with my family this year."

Sierra trotted over. Some of the girls she had been standing with also came over to meet Mitsuko's new friend. They introduced themselves and giggled a lot. Raja didn't catch everything they said, but he caught Sierra winking at Mitsuko and whispering, "You're lucky, Mitsuko. He's cute!"

All of these girls were wearing jeans. Raja looked around and saw that nearly every girl going into or coming out of the school was also wearing jeans. Of course, most of the boys were, too, but Raja was a little uncomfortable. It was not proper in India for girls to show off their legs, even if they were covered by denim. And these American girls certainly were forward!

As they entered the school building and headed for the office, Raja noticed that some of the students were looking at him and pointing.

"Are they laughing at me?" Raja asked anxiously. "You are right, Mitsuko. I am the only one in a uniform. I am sticking out sore like a thumb."

Mitsuko tried hard not to laugh. She guided him into a line of students outside the main office door.

"Tell me about your uniforms, Raja. Do you wear the same thing every day? What do the girls wear in India?" she asked, trying to divert his attention.

"In the school I am attending in India, the boys have blue uniform pants, white shirts and red ties for the days of the week. The girls are wearing blue skirts and white blouses and red ties. On Saturday morning and special days the boys are wearing the same as before but they have also red belts. But the girls then be dressing in white skirts and white blouses with red belts and ties. It would be better here, I am thinking, for me not to be wearing a red tie." Raja tried to make a funny face, so that Mitsuko would think he was not bothered by how he looked.

"You know what, Raja?" she said, taking him by the elbow and moving him a few steps forward in the line. "You look very nice just as you are and I am very proud to walk with you."

Registration was a blur. All Raja could think of was how glad he was Mitsuko was by his side. How would he have managed to find his way around this huge building without her? She helped him as he struggled to understand the questions he was asked. Then she pointed him in the right direction as he moved along the registration table, showed him which papers to sign and which ones to bring home for Mr. and Mrs. Jade to sign, and directed him to the bookstore. As he loaded his books and school supplies into his backpack, he shook his head back and forth.

"These books are so big!" he exclaimed. "In India we are having books only about a half inch thick. There must many more things be to learn in these American books."

"Well, you don't have the easiest courses, you know," she said, laughing. She unfolded his schedule. "Let's see, first hour you have American History. Then, Biology II, followed by Algebra II, and then English. Whew, Raja! You'll be worn out by lunch! Then after lunch, you have Business, followed by a study hall, and then PE. So, what do you think, Raja?"

"I am thinking I will be, how do you say, OK with the math and science. These are things I am being very good at in India. English will be much difficult for me and also the American History for I will be learning about your country instead of mine. But, Mitsuko, what is PE?"

"That is physical education. It's fun, actually. You exercise or swim or play volleyball or basketball."

"We do this also in India, playing games with our friends. It is outside and there is no teacher. It is a kind of free time."

"Well, here in America, you will have PE outside until the weather is bad, and then you will work out in the gym during the winter or if it's raining. But it's a real class and not just a free time. PE is taught by a teacher and you will be given a grade."

"A grade for having fun? This is a strange country!" Raja said, laughing. Then he looked around him. Their footsteps echoed in the long, darkened hallways.

"How will I find all my classes, Mitsuko? How will I know where to go or when I am to be somewhere?" Raja was overwhelmed by the size of the building and the many classrooms that all looked alike.

"It's not that bad, Raja," Mitsuko said, grabbing him by the arm and tugging him toward the stairs. "Your room numbers are right by your course titles, see? Just remember that any room that starts with a 1, like this one, 134, is on the first floor. The ones that start with a 2, like your biology and algebra classrooms, are upstairs on the second floor. They go in order, too, one after the other, even numbers on one side, odd numbers on the other."

She then led him around the entire building, giving him a tour like she had done Saturday around the neighborhood. When they had finished and arrived back to the main entrance, she handed him the schedule and said, "OK, Raja, now we do it again. This time you show me around."

By this time, Raja had forgotten all about feeling out of place in his uniform and red tie. He still felt a little overwhelmed and flushed, but he was enjoying himself immensely. How many other exchange students had a pretty, fun tour guide like Mitsuko to show them around? He was having so much fun he hardly noticed her jeans anymore.

There was one room they had not yet visited, the

gym. Raja was stunned by the size of the "room" where he would have PE. As they entered the gym, someone threw a basketball at Raja and yelled, "Catch!" Raja whirled around and snagged the basketball in one hand, then bounced it across the floor toward the boy who had thrown it. His backpack jostled up and down on his back, but his coordination and the ease with which he handled the ball were not lost on the boys as he approached. Mitsuko trotted alongside him and waved at one boy in particular. He was tall with a light brown crewcut and a friendly smile.

"Hi, Phil!" she called out. "Meet Raja!"

"Nice catch, Raja," Phil said, extending his hand in greeting. "Nice to meet you, too. How about shooting some hoops with us?"

Raja glanced questioningly at Mitsuko. She grinned and reached for his backpack. As he shrugged out of it, he wondered how she would be able to carry something so heavy. But she hoisted it easily over her shoulder and held her arm out for his jacket. He passed that to her and still she stood there waiting.

"Raja," she said at last. "You might want to lose the tie, too."

Actually, he did not want to lose his prized red tie at all, but he had a pretty good idea that this was another one of Mitsuko's expressions—like the chicken coop and goose bumps. He was picking up on these odd American expressions after all. He loosened his tie and tossed it to Mitsuko. Then, unbuttoning his shirt collar, he turned toward Phil and enthusiastically jumped into the game.

"You're good, Raja. Maybe you should try out for the team." Later that night as he lay in bed, he could still hear Phil's words echoing in his mind. He had made a friend today, and all because of Mitsuko. The last thing he remembered as he drifted to sleep was Mitsuko's cheer from the bleachers, "Go, Raja!"

Holy Cow!

Raja was the first one in the kitchen Tuesday morning. He was up even earlier than Brad, who liked to run in the mornings or work out in the gym. Brad hurriedly drank a glass of orange juice and then slapped Raja on the shoulder as he headed out the door. "Have a good day at school, Raja," he said. Before the screen door could snap shut, he poked his head back in and added, "I'll probably see you in study hall this afternoon."

Mom and Dad Jade also wished him well as they ate breakfast and then drove away to their car dealership. Mom handed him the papers they had signed. "If you have any questions, Raja, you just head for the office and ask someone there to help you, OK?" she said kindly. Raja recognized the look on her face. He had sometimes seen it on his mother's face—a blend of worry, concern and confidence. It made him glad to have the Jades as his host parents.

Although it seemed strange to walk with a girl, he was also glad that Mitsuko was walking with him this morning. She had already helped him bridge the cultural gap in a hundred small ways. Raja had decided to wear his uniform pants and shirt this morning, since that was what he had the most of in the way of school clothes. He had left the red tie home, however.

The yellow-haired girl named Sierra joined them at the corner. She talked incessantly and had an annoying habit of whipping her head back to flip her hair out of her face. Raja realized that even though she was supposedly talking to Mitsuko, she kept glancing at him. Then she would giggle and ask too many questions too fast, but she wouldn't give Raja or Mitsuko time to answer. Raja couldn't understand what Mitsuko saw in her.

As they neared the school, he could hear friends calling back and forth to each other, laughing together, and renewing friendships after their summer vacations. The noise and laughter reminded him of the way it was in India on the first day of school. Suddenly he was struck with just how far away from home he really was. He hadn't even been in America a week, but it seemed like such a long time since he had been among his own friends at school.

His attention was brought back to the present by the sound of Mitsuko's voice. Somehow they had made it inside and were standing outside Room 101. Students rushed by in the hallway. There was the sound of locker doors being opened and shut, of footsteps on the shiny linoleum floors, of joking and shouts and laughter.

"OK, Raja," Mitsuko said, tugging on his sleeve to get his attention. "This is the room you'll be in for American history. When the bell rings, you better be in your seat. When it rings again, you have five minutes to get to your next class. Don't horse around and be late either. Remember to match your schedule numbers with those on the doors. Good luck," she called as she turned the corner and headed for her class. Then she was poking her head around the corner again, just as Brad had done earlier that morning. "Raja, we have the same lunch period. I'll try to look for you then, OK?"

"OK," he said, more bravely than he felt. He would be sure not to "horse around," whatever that meant. It probably had something to do with chickens and geese, though.

His legs trembled as he opened the door to Room 101 and cautiously walked in. Although it was noisy inside and students were moving around, the first thing that grabbed his attention was the straight rows of individual desks, all evenly spaced and made of something polished and smooth. He was used to rough benches in India where many students could crowd closely together. But these were single desks! Only one person could fit in each of these! And there couldn't be more than thirty of them. Only thirty students in a room? In India they could get seventy students or more on the benches jammed into the room! There was so much wasted space between these American desks.

While he was staring in amazement, wondering where he was to sit, someone called to him, "Raja, over here."

He turned in the direction of the voice. A boy with skin even darker than Raja's was smiling at him and tapping the empty desk next to him. "You can sit next to me," he said, loud enough to be heard over the noise of the students.

Raja returned the boy's smile and hurried over.

"How you knowing my name?" Raja asked,

extending his hand in greeting.

"Phil told me to be on the look out for you. My name is Steve." He shook Raja's hand. "I'm an international student, too, originally from Uganda. I've lived in America for two years." Nodding in the direction of the desk next to his, he added, "Better get settled in before someone else takes it."

Raja's idea of getting "settled in" was to hoist his backpack on the desktop, fold his long frame into the small desk, and then scoot it noisily across the aisle until his desk was touching Steve's.

"There," Raja said triumphantly, "this is being much better, yes? Just like in India! We are liking to sit close together with our friends so that we can be touching them." Raja felt such relief that he had another new friend, one who was like him in many ways. Steve was looking at him a little strangely, trying to say something. But all Raja could hear was his heart singing, "I have a friend!"

Then he finally heard the laughter.

It started out as a smothered giggle, then got louder as it spread across the entire room. Raja looked around and realized that everyone was laughing at him. This was the last thing he wanted!

Steve was not laughing, however.

"What I am doing wrong, Steve?" Raja asked tragically.

"Hey, easy, Raja," Steve said, reaching across and punching Raja lightly on the arm. He then stood up and glared at the other students. Steve was tall and muscular and it was obvious nobody was going to mess with him.

"Don't pay attention to them," he said loud enough for everyone in the class to hear. Then he indicated that Raja should get up and move his desk back to its original position. "You want to be careful about touching people in America, Raja," he said quietly, so that only Raja could hear. "You'll learn what's appropriate. Like, when I punched you just now, that's an OK touch. That's a guy thing. And you have to remember not to sit too close to someone, unless they say it's OK, or let's say you're at a game and we're all jammed together on the bleachers. You'll figure it out."

There was the sudden scurry of students rushing to their desks as the first bell rang. At the same time an older woman walked in the door and headed for the desk at the front of the room. Raja immediately stood at attention and said loudly but politely, "Good morning, Madam."

When the laughter began again, he nervously glanced around and realized that he was the only student standing. No, wait. Steve was slowly rising from his desk and coming to attention, too. Raja was full of mixed emotions. By the laughter all around him, he knew he must have done something wrong. But when was courtesy wrong? And why didn't American students stand and greet their teacher? Where Raja attended school in India, all students stood and greeted the teacher or any adult who entered the room. Students were to remain standing until the teacher gave them permission to sit. And the students were to stand again when the teacher or adult departed the room.

But only he and Steve were standing now, and the

other students were laughing at them.

"Quiet!" the teacher announced. The room was suddenly silent. There wasn't even the sound of paper rustling. "Gentlemen, thank you for being so polite. You may sit down now." She took a few moments to look over her roster. Then she came around to the front of her desk. "My name is Miss Brown. Steve, I remember you from study hall last year. And your friend must be Raja Shah, an exchange student visiting us this year from India."

Raja smiled and nodded. He liked the way she was speaking so carefully and distinctly.

"Before I take attendance, class," Miss Brown continued, walking up and down the aisles between the desks, "I must say I rather like Raja's very courteous gesture. We could all use a lesson in respect for one another and especially for adults, so from now on when I come into the room, you will all stand and say, 'Good morning, Madam.'"

The students collectively groaned, but Raja smiled when he realized he had won a point for his culture. He looked at Steve, who was grinning back at him.

After attendance, Miss Brown began to write on the blackboard. Raja pulled his copybook out of his backpack and began to copy down everything. He knew how important keeping good notes would be. He must memorize everything so that he would receive a high score on the final exam. Raja could read and write English well and had no trouble copying the blackboard notes, but he had some difficulty following everything

Miss Brown was saying. As various students asked or answered questions, it seemed that Miss Brown was speaking more rapidly than before. He listened carefully, straining to catch every word. In the English medium school he had attended in India, English was spoken. But the sentence structure and word pronunciation differed from what he was hearing now.

Miss Brown noticed the perplexed look on Raja's face and asked, "Do you understand, Raja?"

"Could you be repeating that again, Miss Brown?" he asked.

She repeated herself slowly and distinctly. Then she asked Raja, "Did you understand that time?"

Raja shook his head as he copied notes. Miss Brown then said the sentence again and was about to ask him if he understood, when he suddenly realized what he was doing.

"Yes, yes, Miss Brown, I understand," he said apologetically. "I am sorry and you are not having to repeat it again. In India, to shake the head is to say 'yes.'"

"Well, that is most interesting, Raja," she said, smiling. "But you may want to say 'yes' the American way, with a nod, to avoid a lot of confusion!"

Raja jumped at the sound of the bell, but he was glad to see that he was not the only one. As students began to get up and leave, Miss Brown crossed her arms over her chest and tapped her right foot on the floor. The students looked around sheepishly and then one after another stood at attention by their desks. Raja, standing straight and tall, led the students as they announced, "Good-bye, Madam."

There was hardly a giggle as Miss Brown left the room.

In the hallway, Raja was again overwhelmed by the noise and seeming confusion all around him. In his school in India, the students walked quietly down the hall single file. Steve tapped him on the shoulder, startling him.

"Sorry, buddy," Steve said. "Where's your next class?"

"Biology II in Room 236, I think," Raja said, panicking for a moment as he tried to remember where he had put his schedule. He found it in a side pouch of his backpack.

Steve looked it over as they walked together. "OK, I'll take you there. I'll be just down the hall from you. Looks like you've got Algebra II after that, which is just a few rooms over on the other side. I'll be downstairs that hour, but I'll have time to check on you first. Phil will be in English class with you, so watch for him. Hey, we've got the same lunch hour, Raja. I'll be on the lookout for you, OK?"

It was good to have a friend lead him through the crowd of students. It had been different yesterday with Mitsuko. The halls had been empty for the most part. But now there were so many students and so much noise and he was confused. He knew Steve was going out of his way for him. He wondered if someone had been such a friend to Steve two years ago when he came over from Uganda. Could it have been Phil? Raja hoped he would be able to do the same for someone else someday. That was the way friendship was supposed to work, wasn't it?

By lunch period, Raja was feeling lightheaded. He couldn't imagine how he would ever remember everything he had learned this morning. His copybook was already nearly full of notes! If every day were like this one, he would need many more copybooks.

Steve kept his word and checked up on him after biology and algebra. Then Phil spotted him in English and saved a desk next to him. Before heading to his next class, Phil led Raja to the cafeteria and "handed him off," as he jokingly put it, to Steve again. This was one expression that Raja understood and he enjoyed laughing with Phil and Steve. He felt like "one of the guys," another expression he had picked up on this eventful day.

But now there was another event to consider—lunch. Which meant eating more American food. Raja braced himself. He was certainly hungry enough, but he was not yet used to the strange flavors and textures of food in this country. One thing was immediately apparent as he followed Steve into the huge cafeteria. They would not be going outside to eat. Nor would they be purchasing something from the "walla-walla" rickshaw that normally parked outside the schoolyard gate in India.

Raja was amazed at the seemingly endless rows of tables crowded with laughing, talking students. On the one hand, it was good to see students sitting close together as they did in India. But there was so much noise! Raja felt another surge of panic and hung close to Steve. He was determined to carefully watch everything Steve did and then do exactly the same. He didn't want to be laughed at again.

He picked up a tray and silverware, then studied how students were selecting various items of food and putting them into the compartments of their trays. The line split and students worked both sides of the counter. Steve was now across from him. First Steve picked up an odd little waxed carton. Raja picked one up, too, and read the words on the side. Oh no. Not more of the dreaded American milk! Was there no escaping this terrible drink? Steve had picked a carton with brown colors instead of red colors, so Raja chose the same kind. Chocolate milk, the carton read. Hmmm. Well, Raja would just have to give it a try. It certainly couldn't be any worse than the other kind. Raja redirected his attention to the food items on the serving counter. He thought if he tried everything, then he might find something he liked. He scooped some peaches into one compartment, then some salad in another.

"Steve, where is the rice?" Every meal in India included rice. Mom Jade had even served it several times since his arrival.

"Nope, no rice today, Raja," Steve said. "Actually, we seldom have rice here. But you might like some French fries. Over there, Raja. Put some ketchup on the side. That's it. Now you're talking."

Raja was starting to enjoy himself. It was fun picking out your own food. He looked over at the next bin and saw something very familiar.

"Ah, Steve! Look, you have 'poori' here?" Raja said brightly.

Steve raised an eyebrow as Raja indicated the hamburger buns. "Poori? OK, if you say so! Here we call them hamburger buns. And right next to them are the hamburgers."

Raja watched each student use tongs to pick up what looked like a piece of meat and then place it on a "poori."

"What is hamburger?" Raja asked.

"The all-American staple, my friend," Steve said with a broad grin. "It's ground beef."

For a moment the world stood still. Then Raja inhaled sharply. "Beef? Steve, you are meaning beef that comes from cows?"

"That's the only kind I know of," Steve replied, adding a slice of cheese to his hamburger.

"But we do not eat beef in India," Raja said solemnly. "In India cows are considered to be holy."

Steve looked at Raja and cocked his head to one side.

"No beef, huh?" he said in surprise. "No hamburgers? Holy cow, Raja, you're missing a lot!" Then his eyes widened as he realized what he had just said. "Oh, I'm sorry. No pun intended."

Raja was still studying the bin of beef patties before him. He'd completely missed Steve's remark.

"Hey, could you hurry it up down there?" someone

at the back of the line was grumbling.

"Well, Raja," Steve said, lifting his tray and heading away from the serving counter, "it's up to you, but you're in America now. You might want to learn to eat beef."

I better try a hamburger, Raja thought, or I will never fit in here. I do not want them laughing at me for being different. His hand shook as he reached for the tongs and placed a hamburger patty on a "poori." He watched as other students added lettuce, tomatoes, onions, pickles, mustard and ketchup to their hamburgers and then topped their creation with another "poori." That looks easy enough, he thought. He quickly added the same ingredients to his sandwich. As he neared the end of the serving counter, he spotted a bin of applesauce. He liked applesauce, so he scooped up a generous spoonful and poured it all over his hamburger.

I better try a hamburger, Raja thought, or I will never fit in here.

Just then, someone pointed and said, "Look, that guy just dumped applesauce on his hamburger!"

The all too familiar sound of laughter surrounded him again and he turned away abruptly. He suddenly felt so alone in this huge crowd. And he didn't see Steve anywhere. The tables were full and everyone seemed to be sitting with friends. But where would he sit? In India he was used to having many friends. In fact, he was popular there. He was considered to be a natural leader. Not so in America. Here he was laughed at.

I must find a way to make friends, he resolved. I must do it myself, without having to be "handed off" by Steve or Phil. He walked slowly toward a table where a group of boys seemed to be having a good time.

Balancing his tray in one hand, he reached over and placed his other hand on a boy's shoulder. "May I sit with you?" he asked politely.

The boy pulled roughly away and said, "What are you, weird?"

Raja nearly spilled his tray. He suddenly remembered what Steve had said in American history class that morning. These boys were sitting close together on a bench, like boys in India did. This must be one of those appropriate situations. Then he wondered if maybe he should have punched this boy in the arm instead. Somehow that didn't seem appropriate. I must remember not to do this again, he told himself as he turned and walked away.

Just then, he heard a familiar voice, "Over here, Raja! Come and sit with us."

The familiar face of Mitsuko materialized in the crowd of faces around him. She was waving at him from a table to his left. As he approached, the boys and girls sitting together shifted along the bench to make room for him. He maneuvered his long legs over the bench and then under the table and sat down. Although in India the girls and boys did not sit together, he was happy to be included in Mitsuko's group of friends. He recognized a couple of the girls, including Sierra, who was giggling and staring intently at him.

Mitsuko introduced him to the others as he began to eat. "Finally, I get to sit by you," Sierra said, batting her eyes.

Even if he wasn't thrilled about the way Sierra kept looking at him, it felt good to be crowded together on the bench. He listened closely to the conversations around him, trying to understand at least the basic ideas. They talked so fast, but Raja thought he was beginning to catch on.

It wasn't until he was halfway through study hall that he realized he had eaten his first hamburger—"poori," sacred cow, applesauce and all. And, better yet, he'd learned the best way to solve his dislike of American milk. He leaned over and whispered to Brad, who had saved a desk for him, "Do you think Mom would buy the cartons with the brown colors?"

Brad looked puzzled for a moment, then broke into a huge smile. "Ah, Raja, I see you've discovered chocolate milk!" he said, chuckling.

Working Hands, Praying Hands

R aja was very happy to be in this class called PE. His group had been playing soccer all week in a field behind the school. Raja quickly proved his skill as a player. By Wednesday his name was called first when the team captains made their choices. No one was laughing at him now.

Phil met him Thursday after PE class and invited him to play basketball in the gym. "I hear that shooting hoops isn't your only talent, Raja," Phil said. Steve had joined them by then. "Yeah, the word's out that you've been tearing up some turf on the soccer field," Steve commented, sinking his shot.

"Tearing up turf" sounded to Raja like something he probably shouldn't be doing, but he could tell by Steve and Phil's faces that he was being complimented. He figured it was just another one of those curious American expressions. He thought that perhaps he could fill a copybook with these interesting phrases.

Later, as he walked with Steve down the hallway, he

spotted a man pushing a long-handled device of some kind along the smooth, polished linoleum.

"What he is doing?" he asked Steve.

"That's one of the janitors, Raja," Steve answered. "He cleans the school. You have cleaning people in India, don't you?"

"Yes, but we are not having such clean schools as you have. Your walls are very much nice. In India we have to, ah, how do you say, whitewash the walls many times because of the mildew. The cleaning lady cannot keep the mildew from coming back. And your floors are making very shiny and nice."

Steve looked down, as if seeing the floors for the first time. "I guess we're just used to that, Raja. Sometimes you'll see the janitor with a big polishing machine, going back and forth buffing the floor."

"In India, a sweeper woman is cleaning the rooms with only a short-handled broom. She brushes out all the paper the students having been thrown on the floor into the hallway and then out into the schoolyard. You want to be staying away from her because of the big cloud of dust around her. Why your janitor not be making any big cloud of dust?"

"Gee, Raja," Steve answered, scratching his head. "You ask some strange questions. But I guess it's because he's using a dry mop and not a broom, and I think he sprays something on it to keep the dust down. Besides, we're not allowed to throw paper on the floor. We have to put it in the trash containers. Over there, see, there's one."

Raja thought that over. "I see. But in India we do not need so much these trash containers because we have the cows. They are waiting in the schoolyard to be eating the papers the sweeper woman sweeps out there for them. Sometimes they do not wait but are hungry and come walking into the school down the hallways."

Steve was laughing before Raja could finish what he was trying to say, but Raja could tell that Steve was not making fun of him. Raja began to laugh, too. He had to admit this must seem pretty funny to someone who was not from India.

"So, Raja, it's not OK to eat a cow but it's OK to let one gallop down the halls of the school?" Steve was laughing so hard he could barely catch his breath.

"I am understanding now," Raja sputtered, punching Steve playfully in the arm, "why your American hallways are staying so clean. In India, sometimes the sweeper woman gets mad because she is having to sweep not just paper!"

He and Steve were still laughing when they got to the bicycle rack at the side of school. Steve unlocked his bike and walked it on the side away from Raja. When they reached the street where Steve turned off for home, he stopped a moment.

"Hey, Raja, you should get a bike. Then we could ride together sometimes. I could take you out to the country and you could see how American cows live."

As Raja watched Steve ride away, he thought how good it was to have made such a friend as Steve this week. And he had other friends, too. There was Phil, and Miss Brown, and of course Brad and Mitsuko. And he probably should include Sierra too. Raja walked briskly to the Jade home. Better not to think of Sierra. Much better to think of some way to get himself a bicycle.

Raja woke with a start on Saturday morning when he heard a sound outside his window. He jumped out of bed and looked down from his window. Mitsuko was below, moving some kind of loud, buzzing machine back and forth across the front yard. Was this a floor polishing machine like the janitor used? He knocked on the glass of the window, but she did not see or hear him. He dressed quickly and rushed downstairs.

When he started to come right up to Mitsuko, she quickly let go of the handle bar and held up a warning hand. The machine stopped the second she released the handle bar, but Mitsuko had that serious look on her face again. It was the look he remembered from last Saturday when he had nearly been hit by a car. Raja wondered what he had done wrong now. Mitsuko wasted no time filling him in on the details.

"Raja! Don't ever do that again, do you understand?" she cried out, shaking a finger at him.

For someone so small, she certainly knew how to strike terror into his heart!

"Mitsuko, I am sorry," he said. He paused a moment. "But what am I being sorry for?"

She took a deep breath and released it.

"No, Raja, I am sorry. You don't understand, do

you? This is a lawnmower and I am cutting the grass. We do that in America to keep the grass from getting too tall." She approached him and turned him so that he would have a better view of the lawnmower. Then she pushed down on the handle, lifting the base of the mower. "Look under the mower, Raja. Do you see those blades? When this machine is running, those blades whip around incredibly fast and can cut more than just grass. People lose fingers and toes all the time when they get careless. Look at you. You're still wearing your slippers. The way you were coming at me, you could have gotten your foot caught under there."

"I am seeing now," Raja said quietly. "I could be losing my toes."

"Terrible mess on the lawn, too," Mitsuko quipped, breaking into a grin at last.

"We don't have lawnmowers in my country because we don't have lawns," Raja explained. "If there is any grass in the small places between the houses, the cows come and eat it. So I am thinking the cows are the lawn mowers in India."

Mitsuko laughed. "Hey, why don't you put on some shoes and I'll show you how to mow grass?"

Mitsuko was a good teacher, explaining how to pull the cord, showing him how to adjust the engine speed, and demonstrating the proper way to walk behind the mower and direct it. She even explained how to mow so that you could create a pattern on the grass, with nice even lines. This week she was using an angled pattern. As a precaution, she made Raja release the handle bar several times, so that she was confident he knew how to stop the mower immediately.

This is easy, Raja thought as he cut his first row across the lawn. He completed the front yard and then offered to do the backyard. By the time he finished, perspiration ran in little rivulets down his dusty face.

"Good job, Raja," Mitsuko called from the back steps. "You've earned some lemonade."

How good it felt to finally sit down! "That is harder work than I thought," he said, as he wiped the perspiration from his forehead with the back of his hand. "See, Mitsuko, no goose bumps today!"

Side by side on the steps, they talked and drank their lemonade. Raja thought he had never smelled anything as wonderful as freshly mowed grass. And he enjoyed the gentle breeze tickling his face and cooling him down.

He glanced sideways at Mitsuko as she chattered and he thought, I am enjoying sitting and talking with Mitsuko, but what would my parents think if they could see me now?

That evening at the table, Dad mentioned how nice the lawn looked. Mitsuko proudly described how she had taught Raja to use the lawnmower.

Dad said, "Ah, so now we have three possible mowers in the family! That is good to know. We still have several weeks of mowing to do before the cold sets in, and this family is so busy with activities, sometimes we have a hard time getting someone to mow. Raja, I will appreciate if you will pitch in from time to time. And I'll pay you $10 each time you mow, just as I pay Brad and Mitsuko."

Suddenly, Raja had an idea.

"Dad, would it be possible for me to be doing the mowing every week?" he asked. Dad looked at Mitsuko, who shrugged as if she didn't mind. Then he looked at Brad, who grinned broadly and said, "No problem here!"

"Looks like you've got yourself a job, Raja," Dad said. "But why are you so eager to do this?"

Raja took a long sip of chocolate milk. "I am wanting to buy bicycle to go riding with Steve to see American cows in the country and I will need money for that. Ten American dollars is maybe 300 Indian rupees. How many rupees will I need to buy American bicycle?"

Dad Jade thought for a moment and answered, "Well, Raja, you'll want to save about 100 American dollars. I'll let you figure out the equivalent in rupees, OK?"

Brad was rising from the table when he suddenly had a thought. "Hey, Raja, Mr. Townsend next door asked me the other day if I knew someone who would mow his lawn. You might want to talk to him about that. Their grass looks pretty tall so I don't think they've found anyone yet."

"That would making me have more rupees faster, yes?" Raja inquired.

"Absolutely, Raja," Dad answered. "And with

winter just around the corner, you'll be running out of bicycle-riding weather before you know it. By the way, you may use our mower for any other jobs you pick up."

"Thank you, Dad," Raja said, trying hard to keep his grin from stretching his face out of shape. "But I will pay for the fuel and keeping care of the lawnmower."

Dad nodded thoughtfully, then glanced at Mitsuko and Brad with an arched eyebrow. It was clear that he appreciated what Raja had just come up with all by himself.

That night as Raja knelt to pray, he realized with a pang of remorse that he had skipped his morning Bible reading and prayer time. He had been in such a hurry to get downstairs, he had forgotten to thank the One responsible for getting him to America in the first place. Raja asked God to forgive him for his oversight. As he folded his hands in prayer, he noticed a small blister on his thumb. He must have gotten it from pressing the handle bar so hard. He remembered Mitsuko's stern warning about the mower blades and he thanked God for protecting him from losing his toes.

As he prayed, moonlight spilled into his room and encased him in its gentle glow. Studying his hands, he remembered a time long ago when he was a very small child. He couldn't remember all the details, but he knew he had some kind of condition that the doctors could not heal. His mother and father had taken him to many doctors and they had tried many things, but still Raja's hands were cracked and sore. Sometimes the cracks would bleed. Fingering the small blister on his thumb, Raja remembered very clearly how one evening his mother had placed her smooth, lovely hands over his and prayed for healing.

"Please, God, heal Raja's hands so they do not hurt him anymore," she had prayed simply and sincerely. And in the morning, Raja's hands were healed. He never had any trouble with them again.

Reminded of how God had worked in the past, Raja now thanked Him again and prayed a special blessing on his mother, whose strong faith was such an example to him. He unfolded his hands and opened them before him, turning them over and studying them in the moonlight. He promised God that he would always use his hands in a way that would bring Him honor.

A Great Adventure

Although Raja had never had a paying job before, he threw himself into his lawn mowing with great enthusiasm. He even turned down offers to play soccer and basketball with his friends on Saturdays, so that he could devote himself to mowing grass. Mom Jade found a flannel shirt and a pair of jeans for him to wear when he was mowing and Dad bought him a pair of work boots for protection.

Mr. Townsend was so impressed with Raja's courteous manner and attention to detail that he recommended Raja to another neighbor down the street, Mr. Murdock. On the third Saturday that Raja mowed, he was just beginning to cut Mr. Murdock's lawn when the mower stopped. Raja pulled and pulled on the starter cord, but the machine would not start. He knew there was enough gasoline inside, so he decided it must need more oil. After he had filled the oil tank, he successfully started the mower. But as he mowed, a cloud of blue smoke engulfed him as he trudged around the lawn behind the mower.

One neighbor who was walking her dog laughed at him and called out, "Should I call the fire department?" She did not stop to help him, though, but just kept walking. Someone else was looking at him through a window across the street. That person was laughing too. Was it because of the color of his skin? Most of the students at school had accepted him, but he sometimes got strange looks from adults who did not know him.

Well, there was one thing he knew for sure. The mower should not be pumping out this blue smoke. Raja dropped the bar and the mower shut off. Dad Jade was home this afternoon. He and Mom were doing paperwork in the family room. Raja pushed the mower down the sidewalk and felt a sense of dread. What if he had ruined the mower? He did not have enough rupees yet to buy another lawnmower and he was sure a lawnmower would cost many more rupees than a bicycle. How would Dad react to this? While Raja explained what had happened, Dad listened patiently. Then he rose from his desk in the corner of the family room. "Raja, I am glad you came to me and didn't try to hide this or pretend it was someone else's fault. Come on, let's just check it out, why don't we?"

In the garage, Dad looked the mower over carefully and smiled. "Hey, it's not a big thing, Raja. You just added too much oil. Let's pour some of it out and wipe the excess up. I'll show you the mark you should use as a guide when filling it again, OK?"

"Ah, that is good, Dad," Raja said, sighing audibly.

"I am, how you say, back in the business again?"

That night, Raja took his mowing money from an envelope in his nightstand drawer and spread it out on the bed cover. He counted it over and over again. One lawn on the first Saturday was $10. One dollar of that went into the offering plate on the following Sunday. Three lawns on the second Saturday made $30. He had spent $5 on gasoline and $2 on oil, and put $3 in the offering plate. Today he had made another $30! He would put $3 in the offering plate tomorrow. That left him with $56 American dollars or 1680 rupees! He could hardly believe it! By next Saturday he would have $86 American dollars! No, $83, because he would deduct $3 for the offering plate. He would only have to mow one more Saturday after that to go over $100! Even if he had to buy more gas and oil, he should still have enough for a bicycle.

Of course, he would continue to mow until the grass did not grow. He would keep his commitment to Dad and to the two neighbors. The extra money would be a good thing to have for such things as American clothes or gifts to send home to his family at Christmas. Mr. Murdock had even asked him today if he would consider shoveling their driveway this winter. Raja had to remember to ask Dad about that. In India shoveling usually meant cleaning up after a cow. But he had not seen any cows in Mr. Murdock's yard.

For the past two Saturdays, Steve had stopped by to watch Raja mow. He even mowed for him once in a while to give Raja time to rest.

One day after school, Raja invited Steve up to his room to show him the money he had earned.

"Hey, Raja," Steve said. "This Saturday you'll have enough to get yourself a decent bike. Why don't I bring my Dad's mower over and help you get done faster? Then maybe Mr. Jade can take you to the bike shop after we finish and we can finally take that ride in the country."

That Saturday they had to force themselves not to hurry as they mowed. All Raja could think of was having his own bicycle at last. Steve had been nice enough to let him ride his bike sometimes. They even rode double, but they couldn't go for long distances like that. Steve also had carefully explained the rules of bicycle safety in America. He told Raja that Uganda was like India. Many people rode bikes and people darted in and out of traffic. In America you could not do such things.

Dad pretended to be reading the newspaper when Steve and Raja ran breathlessly into the family room after putting away their mowers.

"Hmmm, you boys certainly are back early," he said, trying to hide his smile behind the paper. "Is there something I can help you with?"

"Dad, you are promising to the bicycle shop go for buying with rupees and I need Steve to show me—" Raja's words tumbled all over themselves in his excitement.

"OK, OK, OK," Mr. Jade said, chuckling as he rose from the recliner. "Why don't we see what kind of bike we can get with your rupees, Raja? I'm glad Steve is coming along, too. He'll make sure I don't make you buy an 'old fogy' bike."

Raja glanced curiously at Steve, who was smiling back at Dad. He didn't know what an 'old fogy' bike was, but he was glad Steve was coming along to share in this special occasion.

The fifteen-minute drive seemed like an eternity. So many red lights today, of all days! And that truck in front of them was going so slow! Would they never get there?

At last they arrived and Raja was suddenly very nervous. He hung close to Dad as they entered the busy shop. He'd never seen so many new bicycles before! Rows and rows of them, their bright colors and silver chrome seeming to sparkle under the store's many fluorescent lights.

Raja stood there like someone in shock. He didn't know where to start. Dad was over on the side talking to a salesman. And Steve was already examining a bike in the fourth row. He moved up and down the aisles like a seasoned veteran, knowing exactly what he was looking for.

"Over here, Raja," he called out, gesturing energetically. "Check out this baby!"

Raja followed Steve around like a puppy. There were many "babies" to check over. Steve pointed out various features to look for in their price range. Dad mentioned safety features as well. And, of course, there was the all-important matter of color.

After about 45 minutes, Raja decided on a blue and silver bike that cost $85. Steve told him it was a good choice and Dad agreed.

Raja's heart seemed to thunder in his chest as he pulled out his wallet and counted the money for the salesman. After all these weeks of saving, it was hard to part with those precious American dollars. They represented the money he had earned from his very first job. He knew how much sweat and hard work had gone into earning them and he had enjoyed counting these American dollars every night. But he also knew that it wasn't the money that mattered. For the briefest moment, he understood what it must be like to experience greed. He had always heard about how much money meant to some people, and how they couldn't get enough of it. Some people even stole it or hurt other people when they took their money away from them.

No, he wouldn't become greedy like that. He knew that money was something that God intended for people to use to provide for their needs and to share with others. That was why Raja was so careful to put a portion of his money into the offering plate for God to use. God also wanted people to use their money carefully and gratefully. He was very happy now to have a bicycle. God liked people to have fun, too!

When he saw Dad and Steve lift his beautiful new bicycle into the back of the station wagon, he was filled with something more than happiness. He felt a real sense of accomplishment! He had earned this bicycle!

He had not been a burden to anyone and had, in fact, helped other people in the process!

Driving home with Dad and Steve, he was so lost in his thoughts, he nearly missed what Dad was saying.

"—very careful when you are riding your bike. You must follow all the traffic rules and go with the traffic, not against it," Dad said.

"Yes, Dad, I promise I will ride in a safe manner always," Raja said, pronouncing the words carefully and meaning every one. He looked behind him at Steve and smiled knowingly. Steve had already proven to be as tough as Mitsuko when it came to safety issues!

When they arrived home, it was still early afternoon. Dad gave them permission to ride a few miles out into the country, if they were home by 5 o'clock. Steve promised to make Raja ride around the neighborhood first to get accustomed to his new bike. As they unloaded Raja's bike and Steve grabbed his from the Jade's garage, Mrs. Jade came out of the kitchen and handed Steve a small cooler.

"I thought you boys might like some snacks for your great adventure," she said. Raja hugged her as Dad secured the cooler with bungee cords to the back of Raja's bike.

And a great adventure it was! Raja's legs were sore that night as he lay in bed, but every ache had been worth it. It had been a beautiful October afternoon in New York. Steve seemed to know the nicest roads. Such wonderful trees with so many colorful leaves! The air had been cool and crisp, hinting at the colder weather to come. But as they rode, the cool air did not bother them and they even removed their jackets after about an hour. In the American countryside there was much more space around the houses. The further out they went, the bigger the spaces were. Miles and miles of green grass, or fields full of American crops like corn. Steve answered all of Raja's questions. And just as he had said, there had been cows! So many! And these cows were all different colors; some were black and white, some brown and white, some dark brown and some completely black. All of them were fat and healthy too, not bony and skinny like so many of the cows that roamed the streets of India. Raja even saw his first pumpkin patch!

In his dreams that night, he felt the wind in his face and heard Steve's laughter in his ear. He felt the

The further out they went, the bigger the spaces were.

comforting shade of the huge oak tree where they had rested, tasted the delicious sandwiches Mom had made them, and smelled the fresh, cool air of the countryside in America. And most of all, he felt the love his host parents had for him and the loyalty and affection of his very special friend, Steve.

Indian
Merchant

The aroma of bacon woke Raja early Monday morning. If Mom was frying bacon, then she would be cooking eggs, too. He liked Mom's bacon and eggs very much. He was learning to enjoy many of the things she cooked. American food was not so bad after all. Even with the tempting smells beckoning him, however, he read his Bible verses and got down on his knees to pray.

"Good morning, Mom!" he said a little while later. "You won't believe how hungry I am. How soon I can eat?"

"Sounds like someone's in a hurry to get to school," she said, placing a plate in front of him. She put her palm over his forehead as if feeling for his temperature and grinned. "Are you feeling OK, Raja?"

"Yes, of course," he replied, with a puzzled look on his face.

"Raja, I'm kidding," she explained. "Most teenagers complain about going to school, you know."

He grinned. "But I am riding my bike for the first

time to school and Steve is meeting me at the corner."
He bowed his head and prayed rapidly, then launched
enthusiastically into his breakfast. He couldn't seem to
shovel in the food fast enough.

"Easy, Raja," Mom chided. "If you eat too fast you
really will get sick!"

"But, Mom, see how little I can get on my fork. My
mouth doesn't feel full." He had been used to eating with
his fingers and could fill his mouth more easily that way.

Just then, Brad came in from his morning run. "I'll
ride with you today, Raja, and show you where to put
your bike and how to lock it up. Give me a couple of
minutes to change clothes, OK? Oh, and maybe after
school today, you and Mitsuko can ride over to Leland
High and catch our game."

"I am liking that much," Raja said. "Maybe Steve
will ride with us too. He was a soccer player in
Uganda."

As Brad and Raja raced along the sidewalk, they
heard Mitsuko behind them.

"Wait for me!" she called, jingling the bell on her
bike. Steve joined them at the corner and the four of
them rode together to school. Brad and Mitsuko kept
trying to outdo each other, nudging one another off the
sidewalk or cutting in front of each other.

"You're going to get bugs in your teeth if you don't
wipe that silly grin off your face," Steve hollered as he
pulled alongside Raja. But Raja made a funny face at
Steve and kept on grinning. He was having such fun.
It was good to be with friends, good to be "horsing

around," good to have his very own bike.

Brad demonstrated how to properly lock up Raja's bike at the bike stand. "My dad bought you this chain and lock. It is important for you to lock your bike each day, Raja. I don't know what it's like in India, but here you can't take any chances, OK? If you forget even once, someone may steal your bike and have some fun of their own. You got that?" Brad asked.

"I got that, Brad," Raja replied.

Normally Raja was so involved in his classes that the hours flew by. But not today! He was so excited about his very own bike being parked outside and the prospect of riding to a soccer game with Mitsuko and Steve, that he had a hard time concentrating on his studies. When the last bell rang, he raced outside, afraid that maybe he had dreamed it all up and there would be no bicycle waiting for him. But there it was. Steve had already unlocked his bike and was waiting for him. Mitsuko finally broke away from a circle of friends and joined them. Soon they were tearing across town to Leland High School, with Mitsuko leading the way, laughing and jingling her bicycle bell. With her long, glossy hair bouncing in the wind, Raja thought she was the prettiest girl he had ever seen.

At the game, some of Mitsuko's girlfriends waved them over to sit with them. When Raja saw that a couple of them wanted to sit by him, he wedged himself between Mitsuko and Steve. These forward American girls made him nervous. Besides, he didn't want to sit by any other girl except Mitsuko.

Brad's team easily defeated the Leland team. Afterwards, some of the players milled around on the field. Brad gestured to Steve and Raja to join them.

"Raja and Steve, we're having an informal practice session," Brad explained. "Everyone's still pretty pumped up and we need to let off some steam. Would you like to join us?"

Raja and Steve looked at each other, smiled, and slapped their hands together in a high-five. They didn't need to be asked more than once. Someone tossed a ball at Steve and he deflected it skillfully with the side of his foot, then booted it toward Raja. They were already out on the field when the other team members joined them.

"That's some pretty fancy footwork, Steve," the team captain said, maneuvering into position. His jersey said his name was Joe. "Why didn't you try out for the team?"

Steve slipped around Joe and kicked the ball to Raja. "My parents thought it best for me to stick with just one sport, so I chose basketball. Soccer is so commonplace in Uganda. Everyone can play it. But not everyone has good basketball skills."

Raja was about to kick the ball to Brad when someone shoved him hard, making him lose his balance.

"We don't want any 'Indian Merchant' playing with us!" a heavyset, red-haired boy named Pete growled at him. He said it loud enough for the others to hear.

"Why is this one named Pete pushing me on purpose?" Raja asked Brad, who ran over and offered him a hand up.

"Don't pay any attention to him, OK?" Brad said. "He's got some problems. Just avoid him and focus on us."

Raja continued to play, staying out of Pete's way. He didn't want any more trouble. But since they were playing on the same team, whenever the opportunity arose, he tossed the ball to Pete the same as he did to any of the others. This surprised Pete, who knew that Raja could have chosen someone else. Again and again when the situation called for it, Raja passed the ball to Pete. Before long Pete was tossing the ball back to him. Together they made some impressive plays.

After the practice game, Pete waited around until he found an opportunity to come up to Raja.

"Uh, Raja, about that stuff earlier," he said, digging one foot into the loose dirt at the edge of the field. "I was out of line. No offense?"

"No offense, Pete," Raja said as he reached out to shake hands with Pete.

"Too bad you didn't get to our country earlier, man. You could have made the team," he said and walked away.

"Hey, Indian Merchant, how about we catch something to eat?"

Raja turned to see Phil grinning at him from the sidelines. Mitsuko and Steve were standing with him. Raja figured he'd be stuck with that nickname for the rest of his stay in America. As he joined them, Steve wrapped an arm around his shoulder. "Welcome to the wonderful world of race relations, my friend," he said with a knowing smile on his dark, handsome face.

On Friday, when Raja went to the bike stand to unlock his bike, it was not there. He stood for a moment stunned. No, this couldn't be right. He had put it in the same place every day this week. He had locked it carefully every morning, just as Brad had told him. But there was no mistaking it. His bike was gone.

Frantically, he ran to the other bike stands around the school and searched for his bike. He walked all over the campus and then to the football field, the soccer field, the baseball diamond, even the tennis court. His bike wasn't in any of those racks either.

Mitsuko spotted him walking dejectedly from the tennis court to the parking lot at the side of the school building.

"Raja, what's wrong?" she asked in alarm. She quickly pedaled to him.

"My bike is not here," he said simply. She could read the rest in his face.

"Oh, Raja, are you sure? Where else have you looked?"

He told her everything he had done, all the places he had searched. She questioned him about whether he had made sure the lock was secure, then she jumped off her bike and offered to search with him again.

"I don't know about you, but sometimes I can look right at something and not see it," she said, hoping her voice sounded optimistic.

But despite their best efforts together, Raja's bike was not to be found. They walked home together with Mitsuko's bike between them. Nothing she said this time could make him smile.

When they told Dad what happened, he called the police. An officer arrived as they were eating dinner. Mom offered him a place at the table and the officer sat down, but only accepted a cup of coffee.

Raja had never seen an American policeman up close before. This officer had broad shoulders and was very serious looking. He wore a gun and Raja spotted handcuffs on his belt. Some kind of radio crackled on his shoulder. He turned the volume down and asked Raja several questions, jotting down notes on a clipboard.

Raja had some trouble speaking because he was nervous, but his host family helped him out and kept him calm. The officer was pleased that Raja had his sales receipt with a description of the bike and its serial number.

Before he left he said in a kind voice directed at Raja, "I am sorry to say this happens a lot in our country. But we do recover many bikes. You might want to call us in a week or so to see if we have found it, though. Sometimes we get busy with other cases and it slips our minds. But I will try very hard not to let that happen. We'll keep our eye out for it, Raja, I promise."

When the officer had left, Raja chewed absently on his food. "That was very nice of him to coming here and talk with me. The police in India often pick up bikes they find laying around, but they will never be coming to my house and talk to me about it like this man is doing. Thank you for helping me talk with him. I was not so scared with you here."

Raja was once again walking to school. Steve let him ride double with him sometimes and Mitsuko offered her bike to him. She said they could take turns. Raja said he enjoyed walking and needed the exercise. He didn't want to offend her by telling her he didn't want to ride a girl's bike that had a bell and pink streamers on the handlebars. He couldn't imagine with so many bikes in this city, someone had to steal his beautiful blue and silver bike. He had worked so hard for it. Did someone really steal it or did some of the boys just hide it as a joke? Maybe it was a race relations thing.

A couple of weeks later, Dad said, "Why don't you call the police station and check on your bike? That's what Officer Nelson suggested."

Raja wasn't very comfortable talking on the phone, but he knew it was something he needed to practice. Some of Mitsuko's "forward" girlfriends liked to call him. They giggled at his mispronunciations. That embarrassed him, but Mitsuko said most of the girls thought his English was "cute." He wondered what his parents would think of that!

But for now his thoughts were on carefully pronouncing his words as he spoke to the desk sergeant. After a few repetitions, he finally got the sergeant to understand him.

"Listen, Roger," the sergeant said in a brusque voice. "Might be a good idea for you to just come on down. Our guys collected a few bikes over the weekend and you just might hit the jackpot."

Raja politely thanked the sergeant, even if he had

said his name wrong. Well, Roger was better than Indian Merchant, wasn't it? He didn't know what "hitting the jackpot" was all about, but figured it must be a good thing. After he found out what that was, he needed to remember to write it down in his copybook of American expressions.

Dad was already waiting by the door with his car keys in his hand. Raja smiled at him and pulled on his jacket. It was dark outside and the October nights were getting colder.

At the police station, they were led through the building to a large shed in the back of the fenced-in parking lot. A police officer unlocked the door for them. Inside, Raja saw at least 50 bikes! He and Dad carefully walked through them, pulling them this way and that, checking to see if there was a blue and silver one in the bunch. And there it was!

"Over here, Dad," Raja called out. He was already unfolding his sales receipt and reading off the numbers as Dad held a flashlight against the side of the bike. The police officer confirmed that it was the right bike and then had Dad and Raja sign a release form. They walked the bicycle back through the police station and out the front door and then Dad loaded it into the station wagon.

How different this was from the first time he had seen Dad and Steve load his brand new bike into the station wagon. That day had been one of excitement and wonder. Tonight, he had mixed feelings. He was happy to get his bike back at last, but sad that it had been stolen in the first place.

In the garage at home, Dad checked the bike over carefully. It was dirty and there was a small dent in the front fender. The brakes weren't working either. But it was late and Dad suggested they call it a night. He would show Raja how to repair the brakes after school tomorrow.

"Thank you, Dad, for all you have been doing in helping me. I hope I am not being too much trouble."

Dad turned back and placed both hands on Raja's shoulders. He was a little shorter than Raja and had to look up at him. "Raja," he said. "You are not any trouble at all. We are very proud of you and enjoy having you live with us. I just wish the world was a nicer place and such things did not happen."

"It is not such a bad thing," Raja said. "There are many worse things. We are having our health and many good things and even if there is much bad, God is good."

Mr. Jade nodded thoughtfully. Raja thought he saw a glimmer of something in his eyes.

"You are a wise young man, Raja," he said and his voice was husky with emotion. He gave Raja a quick hug and turned back to the kitchen.

Raja stayed in the garage for a few more minutes, wiping his bicycle with a rag. Outside, the wind was picking up. He knew it was pushing fallen leaves across the empty streets and into the gutters. And he knew that each day was a little colder than the one before. There would not be many more days left in this year for him to ride his beautiful bicycle.

The Essay

Late one Saturday morning in November, Raja was sitting alone at the table in the kitchen working on an assignment. He heard the car pull into the garage. Mom had gone to the grocery store earlier and Raja knew she would need help unloading the groceries. As she walked in, he took the grocery bag she was holding and set it on the table.

"I will get the rest for you, Mom," he said, helping her out of her coat.

"Thank you, Raja," she said. "That's a big help. I'll start putting these away." She noticed that Raja seemed preoccupied. He carried in all the groceries and even helped her put them away, but he was not his usual cheerful self.

"Raja, is everything OK? You seem a little down," she inquired.

"Ah, Mom, it is not for you to worry. I am having to write an essay for Monday and I don't know how to start. Writing English is very hard for me."

Mom had opened a box of cookies and was putting a few on a napkin for him. She reached for the chocolate milk and then put it back suddenly, as if she'd had another idea.

"What topic did your teacher give you?" she asked. She reached for a square, brown can in the cabinet above the stove, then bent down and retrieved a small saucepan and placed it on the front burner of the stove.

"It can be anything that has to do with the holiday season," he replied, watching as she pulled a carton of the dreaded white milk out of the refrigerator. What was Mom doing? She knew he didn't like the white milk. And now she was pouring it into the saucepan and heating it up?

"Why don't you write about your family in India, Raja?" she offered. "I'm sure that the other students will want to hear about them." She spooned out some dark powder from the square can and added it to the milk in the saucepan. Then she added a few spoons of sugar and began stirring.

He picked up his pad and pencil and began to slowly write. Then he looked up nervously. "Mom, the teacher wants us reading our essays in front out loud, and I am needing this to have a good grade. But I'm having trouble writing my sentences in the American way."

Mom poured some of the warm, brown milk into a cup and placed it in front of him. She also dropped in two white things. Raja was intrigued by how they floated on top. "Here, Raja, try some of this. I think you'll like it. Write your paper and then I'll go over it with you later and help you make corrections."

"What this is?" Raja said, taking a careful sip and then smiling broadly.

"We call it hot cocoa. It's something nice and warm to drink on a cold November day. And those are marshmallows on top. You can eat them or just let them melt. So, what do you think?"

"I like this hot cocoa very much, Mom. I am thinking it will help me write better!"

"If I get busy later, Raja, I'm sure Mitsuko will help you, too."

She walked into the laundry room and Raja began to write about his family. As he wrote, thoughts of his father, mother and two sisters caused his heart to ache. Not even the wonderful hot cocoa could keep him from feeling homesick.

My Country and Home
By Raja Shah

India is my home. I traveled 22 hours by train and another 25 by plane to come to America. I am a student here for one year. I have two sisters younger than me. My father has his doctorate, and teaches in college. My mother is a math teacher in a junior college. Since I am the oldest son, it will be my responsibility to take care of my parents in their old age, so it is important for me to get top grades. When I return to India I will need good enough grades to continue my schooling. I am planning to get a master's degree in business someday so that I will have a good job and then be able to care properly for my parents.

Just then, Mitsuko rode up on her bike and jingled her bell outside the kitchen door. Raja jumped up and joined her outside.

"Hey, Raja, want to come with me to watch Brad practice basketball?" Her eyes were bright and her nose was red from the cold. She had on gloves and a sock hat. She was still wearing the jacket she normally wore, but had snapped in a wool lining a couple of weeks earlier.

"I can't," Raja said. "I am having to write an essay for school on Monday. It is very much hard work. Mom said I might want to write about my family in India and I am doing that. Are you having any other ideas?"

"Is this Miss Brown's assignment about holidays?" Mitsuko asked, blowing into her gloves and then rubbing her hands together. Her breath puffed around her face like little clouds.

"Yes. Do you think Mom's idea is good one? " Raja asked.

"Yes, I do," Mitsuko said, thinking Raja's answer over carefully. "Hey, you could compare holidays. You know, how holidays in India differ from holidays in America. Something like that."

"You have a good idea, Mitsuko," said Raja. "I am liking that!"

"So, are you coming or not?" she pressed. When she saw his hesitation, she added. "Raja, it looks like you need a break. And you've got all afternoon to write your essay. Tomorrow afternoon, too, if necessary."

That's all Raja needed to hear. Mitsuko had warned

him to "bundle up," so he dressed in his warmest jacket, and then put on the gloves and hat Mom had given him. Once they had ridden their bikes a few blocks, he began to warm up. This was one way to make those goose bumps "flew the coop"!

Mitsuko didn't know why Raja was laughing all of a sudden, but she jingled her bike bell and laughed with him.

As they were riding home after practice, Raja asked, "Mitsuko, will you read my paper when I finish and help me correct my mistakes?"

"Sure, Raja!" she hollered, pulling ahead of him. "I'd be glad to. Besides, I'm curious to read about your family. You don't talk about them a lot."

As soon as they arrived home, Raja went to his room and began to write at his desk. He had seen many of the Thanksgiving and Christmas decorations around town. Some of the classroom bulletin boards were also decorated. He had not yet experienced firsthand Thanksgiving and Christmas in America, but he had studied about them in India. Some of his American teachers at the English Medium School in India had taught them a few of the American customs. Raja thought all this over as he wrote and he didn't stop until he was called down for supper.

There are many Hindu holidays in India. Hindus worship the cow, so on special days they always decorate cows with flowers, and allow them to wander wherever they want.

The cows sometimes walk up to doors of homes and beg. Then a lady gives them food. They walk in the streets and markets. Sometimes they lie down in the middle of the street. They wander around eating anything they find such as paper scraps and banana peels. They will even eat pages out of books if you leave them lying around.

The government gives Christian people only one day holiday for Christmas. There is no "Christmas Vacation." Their school break is called "Winter Vacation." During Christmas season, you will not hear Christmas music or see Christmas decorations in stores and business places as you do in America. Only in Christian homes will you see signs of Christmas. Many Christians display a star in homes. In this way, as you travel down the streets, you can tell the Christian homes scattered among the Hindu and Moslem homes.

The narrow, dusty streets in my town are crowded with cows, people, motor bikes, and bicycles. Cars are driven on the left side of the street. There are very few cars in my town, but there are some trucks. When classes are over each day, my friends and I ride our bikes. We stay close to each other so we can hold hands or touch a friend's shoulder as we dart in and out among people, cows, and vehicles on the street.

Thanksgiving in my country is different from your celebration. Thanksgiving services are held in churches or chapels. Offerings such as vegetables, chickens, and grain are brought to church and laid on a mat in front of the pastor (padra). While he is speaking, people, young and old, bring what little they have. A small child may bring two or three eggs or a few green beans. You may see a man with a sack of wheat or rice over his shoulder. Live chickens with their feet tied together are brought and laid on the floor. They might squawk while the pastor is speaking, but the service continues anyway. Following service, all the gifts are carried outside. Chairs and benches are set up and preparations are made for an auction. Snacks are served during the auction. This is a big day in the lives of many poor people. They do not keep the money for themselves. They find someone poorer than they are. One particular day when I was there, they chose to give to leprosy patients who had less than they did. This is the way that they showed thankfulness.

After supper, Mitsuko and Raja washed, dried and put away the dishes, while Brad wiped the counters, swept the floor, and carried out the garbage. When they had finished, Raja asked, "Mitsuko, would you have time now to go over my paper and show me where I made mistakes and check to see if my verbs are in the place where they belong? Then I can write over the essay on nice paper tomorrow afternoon."

"Great idea," she said. "Let's get busy."

Raja gathered his papers and brought them down to the kitchen table. Mitsuko read through the essay quickly, but seemed interested in what she was reading. Mom joined them as they worked and read through it as well. She suggested that Raja move the order of some of the paragraphs around. For instance, it might be better to put the paragraphs about the cows and traffic all in one section, then reverse the order of the Thanksgiving and Christmas sections. Mitsuko agreed and Raja nodded. Yes, this made sense to him.

Mitsuko also pointed out some punctuation errors and the places where he had left out little connecting words such as *a*, *an*, or *the*, as well as the endings on some words. Since Raja had written his essay in black ink, she marked her corrections and suggestions in blue ink. "Raja, I think that will do it. If I know you, however," she said, raising her eyebrows slightly, "you'll go upstairs and start rewriting this and work deep into the night."

When he smiled guiltily, she shuffled the pages of the essay into a neat stack and said, "You know, when I write something, I like to let it simmer a bit before I look at it again." He was looking at her oddly, so she rephrased her comment. "What I mean is, I like to get some distance from it, then look at it fresh the next day. It's amazing what new things you'll see if you do that."

Raja nodded.

"Thank you very much, Mitsuko, for doing this for me. You are a very good friend." He'd never said that to a girl before because he'd never had a friend that was a girl. He felt his face flushing again and hoped she wouldn't notice.

But she was smiling that special smile, the one she sometimes smiled when she looked back at him from her bike and then jingled her bell. "That means a lot to me, Raja," she said simply.

On Sunday afternoon, he read his essay in his room and rewrote it, careful to make the corrections Mom and Mitsuko had suggested. That night before he crawled under the covers, he read from his English Bible and then knelt in prayer.

"Please God, take care of my family so far away in India. And help me give my report in a way that gives You and my country honor if I am called on in class. Amen."

Changing Attitudes

Raja jerked awake, afraid for a moment that he had overslept and was late for class. Checking his alarm clock, he saw that he still had fifteen minutes left before his alarm would ring. But he was much too nervous for sleep. Instead, he arose, made his bed, read from his Hindi Bible and prayed for both his families—his Indian family and his American family. After showering, he started to dress in the dark pants and forest green shirt he had picked out the night before, then changed his mind. Something prompted him to wear his uniform today. And not only that. He felt he should wear the red tie, too.

He wanted to look his very best when he stood in front of the class today. Looking at himself in the dresser mirror, he knew his brown skin and dark, curly hair contrasted to his starched white shirt. But he smiled at his reflection in the mirror. This was the way God had made him and if God was happy with His handiwork, then he was happy too. Before he left his room, he turned back and made one more change. Yes, today was definitely a day to wear the red belt too.

He jumped on his bike and headed for school. As always, Steve joined him at the corner. They were among only a handful of students who still rode their bikes to school. Most students found it too cold to ride their bicycles, but Raja and Steve weren't about to surrender to the American cold just yet.

"Whoa, who are you and what have you done to Raja?" Steve quipped when he spotted Raja's red tie peeking up from under his winter jacket.

"You should know, Steve," Raja said, racing ahead. "We are giving our reports today. And I am wanting to, how you say, represent India in a good way."

"Is that what you wrote about?" Steve asked as he pulled up alongside Raja.

"I told about my family and customs in India," Raja answered. "And what did you write?"

"About Christmas shopping on the Internet and how it's nice for handicapped people," Steve said. "I'm learning a lot in my computer class and I thought I'd talk about some of that. My host Mom is wheelchair-bound, you know. She can't get out much."

"No, I am not knowing that, Steve. And that is a more interesting subject than my essay, I am thinking."

"Hey, buddy, don't you worry about that. You'll do fine. Personally, I know that I'm looking forward to hearing about your country."

At that, Raja smiled. It encouraged him to know Steve was interested in what he might have to say. In India, Raja had been used to his fellow students looking up to him. He was comfortable speaking in front of a classroom crowded with seventy or more students. Most of them were his friends and frequently smiled at him as he spoke. But it was so different here in America. Most of the students here still thought of him as an oddity. Many of them laughed when he talked because his English was still so poor.

As he and Steve walked into their American history classroom, he felt a pang of regret for wearing his uniform and tie. Already the giggles and stares had begun. Steve placed a guiding hand on his shoulder and directed him to his desk.

The bell rang and the class stood as Miss Brown entered.

Perhaps they are still angry with me because we have to stand and greet our teacher each morning, he thought. Perhaps they will laugh at me when I have to stand in front of them. His essay rustled in his hands and he looked down to see his hands trembling. A student was already giving her report in front of the class, but Raja had a hard time concentrating on what she was saying. He looked down at his hands again and remembered the way his mother's hands had looked folded over his in prayer. He remembered how God had performed a miracle in his life. If God could do such a big thing then, perhaps He would do a small thing for Raja today.

He bowed his head and prayed silently, "Please, God, help me. I am so afraid." He sensed a calmness pass over him and the trembling in his hands stopped.

A good thing, too, because Miss Brown had just called his name. He walked confidently to the front of the room, but when he turned around to face the class, he nearly panicked. The faces before him registered all kinds of things, none of them pleasant. One boy in the back was smirking. A girl was whispering something to another girl and giggling. Another boy looked angry.

Raja glanced over in Steve's direction. His friend was smiling at him and nodding the way he did when they played soccer together. It was a signal they gave one another when they were ready to move the ball. It meant, "keep your eye on me and let's do this thing together."

Raja took a deep breath, straightened his shoulders and stood tall. He could do this. Hadn't he participated in debates and won many times in India? This was not that much different, he told himself. Clearing his throat, he read out loud, "*My Country and My Home* by Raja Shah."

Although he knew the words were all spelled right, he had trouble pronouncing them correctly. Each time he said a "v" for a "w" sound, or a "d" for a "th" sound, the students glanced around at each other and snickered. Miss Brown cut them off sharply and told Raja to continue. He did, but he noticed that the students made funny faces at him instead. Some of these Miss Brown did not see.

Raja focused his attention on Steve and bravely continued reading. After a paragraph or so, he looked away from Steve and saw that many of the students were no longer grinning or making strange faces. They had begun to listen to his article, really listen. Some of them seemed captivated by Raja's description of Thanksgiving and Christmas in India. When he finished, he bowed politely and was startled to hear applause. Then hands shot up in the air. Raja was already halfway to his desk when Miss Brown called him back to the front of the classroom.

"It appears that your classmates would like to ask you some questions, Raja," she said smiling.

As he faced the class again, he was amazed at the difference in their expressions. There was respect and curiosity and admiration on these faces now. Oddly, Steve was the one smirking now and giving him a thumbs-up. Raja grinned back at him.

"Why are you wearing a red tie and belt today, Raja?" a boy named Tom asked.

Raja explained the custom of wearing uniforms and how the red belt meant today was a special day.

"Does everyone in your country have to stand up when the teacher comes in?" Agnes asked.

"Yes," Raja answered. "In my country, we are taught respect for our teachers and elders. Standing when they enter and leave is one way to show this."

Steve spoke up. "That is the custom in Uganda too. In fact, that is done in many countries. In America, the students get away with much more than is allowed in most schools around the world."

Raja was more certain than ever that Steve was becoming the best friend he had ever had. He thought that even when they each went back to their own countries, they would stay friends.

"Why do you talk so funny?" a boy named Al blurted out.

That question caught him off-guard. He was embarrassed and didn't even notice that someone else had just jabbed Al with an elbow.

"Well," Raja said, faltering a little, "I am trying hard to working on that better. In India, the verbs come at the end of the sentences. Also, I am knowing that I say some sounds different than you are saying them. I am hoping to learn to work my mouth differently so that they come out the right way. I hope you also will help me."

"Do you worship the cow too?" asked a student named Bart.

"No, it is the Hindu people who worship the cow. I am a Christian. I do not worship the cow, but we still must accept having cows in the streets and market places as just the way of life in India. It is good to respect the beliefs of others and for them to be respecting yours too."

That point was not lost on the class. He saw Miss Brown nod thoughtfully.

Steve said, "I like the way you celebrate Thanksgiving. We do much the same in my country of Uganda."

"Thank you, Steve," Miss Brown said. "And thank you, Raja. Excellent report! You may sit down. Class, we can all learn a lesson on how to be thankful from what Raja has told us. Since we will soon be celebrating Thanksgiving Day in this country, your next assignment will be to write a paragraph listing five things you are thankful for."

The students groaned and Al snapped, "First, Raja

makes us stand up when Miss Brown comes in and leaves. Now he's going to change our Thanksgiving customs. Next thing you know, we'll have to wear uniforms to school!"

Raja heard a rumble of laughter around him. Even he was smiling. But Miss Brown was not smiling.

"Al, because of that comment, you will write TEN things you are grateful for in your essay," she chided. "I think it's obvious that Raja is not intending to change anything. I'm sure he will enjoy Thanksgiving turkey as much as you do. He is here to learn about America and we can be courteous enough to try to learn something about his culture too. Now, Steve, I believe your report is next."

Raja watched Steve as he spoke, smiling and nodding as Steve had done for him. But he didn't hear a word he said. He was still flushed from his experience in front of the room. Miss Brown had said "Excellent job." Did that mean he would get a top grade? Would he now make more friends or would they still consider him an oddity? And how could he learn to speak without making people laugh?

Riding home with Steve after school, they chatted about their reports. Most of the trees were bare. The leaves were piled in stacks in the gutters, awaiting pickup by the big garbage trucks that came around once a week. Sometimes they rode over some of the loose leaves on the sidewalk and they made a crunching sound under the tires. The cold, crisp November air was laced with the faint smell of wood smoke curling up from some of the chimneys on the houses.

It was good to be riding and talking with a friend who was like him in so many ways. Raja smiled and waved at Steve as he turned and rode down the street to his home.

He knew as clearly as the cold breeze on his face that Steve would be near the top of his "Thankful List."

There was one Name he would place first on the list, however. He stopped right in the middle of the sidewalk, braced his bicycle against his legs, bowed his head and whispered, "Thank you, God, for helping me today."

Zone Out

Mitsuko and Steve decided to become Raja's speech tutors. The first Saturday morning after Raja and Steve's reports, they set up in the Jade's big dining room. Mrs. Jade had suggested this room because it had a bigger table where they could spread out their books, and because it had more privacy than the kitchen. Mom Jade had referred to the kitchen as "Grand Central Station" these days, an expression Raja didn't quite understand.

Steve had explained, "She means really busy, like La Guardia." Raja finally understood and jotted that phrase down in his copybook of interesting American expressions.

Mom Jade also thought the dining room would be a good place for them to study for the upcoming midterms. "And it's not too far from the food source, either," Mitsuko quipped.

Raja knew he needed help. He was doing well in biology, algebra, and PE. Business and American history were much harder, and English was hardest of all.

"Steve, I do not understand. Why you are speaking English so well?" he asked.

Mom Jade thought the dining room would be a good place for them to study.

"In Uganda I attended an English boarding school from the time I was very small, so speaking English is second nature to me."

"I don't know about you, Steve," Mitsuko piped in, "but I've been in America so long that I think in English now instead of Japanese. I've forgotten most of my native language!"

"It would probably come back to you if you were over there," Steve remarked.

"Yes, I'm sure you're right, but I'm glad I'm here. This is my home, Steve," she said softly. There was a touch of sadness in her tone. Raja wondered what had happened to Mitsuko's parents so long ago and why she had been adopted by an American family. Perhaps someday she would tell them.

Steve sensed the change in Mitsuko. "Hey," he said brightly. "Don't you admire those people who can speak four or five languages fluently? I wonder how they do that?"

Raja chuckled. "I would be happy to learn only one beside my native language. But this English is a hard cookie, is it not?"

"Speaking of cookies," Mom Jade interrupted, coming into the room, "I thought you kids might like a snack." She set a tray down on the table and left. The "kids" grabbed napkins, cookies and glasses of milk and munched happily for a few minutes.

"You know, Raja," Mitsuko finally said, wiping cookie crumbs from her mouth, "I think part of your problem with pronunciation comes from the way you shape your mouth when you are speaking certain words."

"How you mean?" he said. He was chewing a chocolate chip cookie and his voice was muffled. Steve laughed and sputtered cookie crumbs, which made Raja laugh.

"OK, you clowns, let's stop horsing around. If we want to have time to ride our bikes this afternoon, we have to get busy now."

There was more laughing and sputtering but finally Steve and Raja settled down.

Mitsuko continued. "OK, Raja, when I say *this*, where do you see my tongue?"

"It is between your teeth coming out a little," Raja replied.

"All right, now you say *this*, Raja, and tell me where

your tongue is when you say it. Wait," she said, digging around in her purse. She pulled out a compact and opened it. "OK, look into this mirror and say *this*, Raja."

Raja did as she instructed and immediately saw that his tongue did not come out between his teeth, but touched the roof of his mouth instead. In doing so, the word *this* sounded like *dis*. He blinked in surprise and looked up at Steve and Mitsuko.

"OK, Raja, now I want you to watch Steve's mouth when he says *what*. Steve?"

Steve shrugged and said, "What." Mitsuko made him say it again, more slowly.

"Now, Raja," she said, tapping the compact. "You say it."

He looked at his mouth in the tiny mirror and saw that once again he was doing something different with his mouth. He tried a few times more.

"What do you think, Raja?" Mitsuko asked.

"Well, I am thinking that when you say a word with a *w* sound, your mouth is making a little circle, and when I say this word, my upper teeth go over my lower lip instead, and it comes out with a *v* sound."

"So, Raja, what do you have to do to correct that?" she pressed.

"I must be thinking of each word and making my mouth work different, yes?"

"Yes."

Mitsuko pulled out a piece of paper with lists and lists of words she had written earlier. She scribbled a few more words on the sheet of paper and handed it to

Raja. "Now, for the next several minutes, I want you to pronounce these words by practicing what you have just learned. And you have to do it out loud, so we can hear you. Steve is going to help me with my geometry while you do that, OK?"

So, Steve helped Mitsuko work out her geometry problems while Raja stuck his tongue between his teeth and said, "This, that, these, those, them, there, thus, thing, therapy, theater, thanks, through, throttle, throw, thumb, three, thoroughbred, thorn, thrifty . . ."

When he thought his tongue was all stretched out of shape, she plopped another sheet of paper on the table in front of him and gestured for him to continue.

He sighed loudly and then pursed his lips until he was making a little "o."

"What, where, when, why, who, wheat, whisker, whisper, whale—" he began. Every once in a while, his upper teeth would move across his lower lip and he would mispronounce a word. Mitsuko would look up and arch an eyebrow at him, then tap the compact. He would grin apologetically and start over. His mouth felt like it was going to fall off. Mitsuko was a hard teacher.

When Steve had checked all of Mitsuko's geometry problems, they turned back to Raja.

"OK, now we work on sentence structure," she announced. Steve rolled his eyes and yawned, making Raja laugh again.

"You have a tendency to expand your verbs, Raja. Cut that out, Steve. I can see what you are doing. Raja, sometimes you say, 'He is liking chocolate milk,' when all you need to say is, 'He likes chocolate milk.' Also, you need to add more prepositions and articles to fill out your sentences."

"What is preposition and article?" he asked.

"What is *a* preposition? What is *an* article?" she corrected. "The *a* and *an* are articles. They are little words that usually come before a noun. But not always. Prepositions are also little words like *in*, *on*, *over*, *to*, and *at*. We ran *to* the store. *To* is a preposition. *The*, by the way, in that sentence is an article."

She pulled out yet another sheet of paper from her notebook and handed it to him. On both sides of the paper she had written sentence after sentence demonstrating the use of articles and prepositions and verbs. She had written funny sentences about things that had happened around the Jade household, things he would understand.

"The chickens flew out of the coop."

"The blue and silver bike raced through the street like a rocket."

"Does chocolate milk come from brown cows?"

"Just because there is smoke, doesn't mean your mower is on fire."

As he began to read them out loud, he realized how much more interesting these sentences were than the ones in the grammar book. He also realized that Mitsuko had taken a lot of time to do all of this for him. He thought perhaps these handwritten study papers would be more help to him than all of the books he would ever read.

"In India, my father many times gives 'too-shun' to students who are having, ah, who have a hard time with their studies," Raja said.

"Does 'too-shun' mean tutoring?" Mitsuko asked.

"Yes, I think so. And I am thinking you are giving good 'too-shun' to me, Mitsuko. But you are much harder than my father!"

Mitsuko make a funny face. "Because you are such a tough cookie, Raja!"

After lunch, they raced through the neighborhood on their bikes and headed out to the country. It was a sunny day, with a light southwesterly breeze and the temperature in the high 50s. They stopped at the same oak tree Steve had taken Raja on the day he had purchased his bike. This time the tree did not give them any shade because its leaves had long since fallen. It stretched high above them like some solitary, silent soldier watching over them and warning of the harsh winter to come. But the three friends were in a cheerful mood, enjoying each other's company and the sun on their faces as they ate their snacks. They knew it might be the last time they would be able to ride their bicycles before winter arrived, and they wanted to make the most of it.

By the time they pedaled home, thick clouds were building in the east and a sharp wind howled in the tops of the barren trees.

The three friends studied hard over the next several days. Raja had little trouble reading and understanding his assignments, but still had difficulty understanding certain teachers. They seemed to talk too fast for him.

He also had trouble in group discussions. He often had to ask someone to repeat what he or she had said, or to face him and say it again so that he could match their words with the movement of their mouths.

He was especially worried about an American history test the following day. Set up in their usual spots at the dining room table, Steve and Mitsuko worked with him the evening before the test.

"So many new names and places, Steve. How will I remember them all?"

"But you know where they are on the maps, Raja," Steve said. "You're dynamite when it comes to geography. I mean, face it, you know all these new countries emerging in Russia and Africa before they even make it on the map!"

"I have an interest in world events, but I know these places best in my own language. I am not thinking . . . I mean, I do not think fast enough in English to remember the names."

"Ah, Raja," Mitsuko said, with genuine pride on her face. "I don't know how you will do on your test tomorrow, but you just said two sentences in some of the best English I've ever heard!"

That made him smile. Still he could not hold down the surge of fear he felt over this coming test.

As he walked into the classroom with Steve the next morning, Mitsuko hurried up to them. If she was not careful, she would be late for her own class, but she seemed intent on saying something. "Try not to worry, Raja," she said, looking up at him. "Just do your best and it will be all right." Then she was racing around the corner and up the stairs to her class.

Miss Brown seemed very stern this morning as she handed out a blue booklet and a single sheet of paper.

"Leave your papers turned over until I say it is time to begin," she said in a serious tone. At the signal to begin, Raja turned his paper over. Up to this point, Miss Brown had given them essay assignments and a few pop quizzes. He wrote the essays at home and had them checked by Mom Jade or Mitsuko. The pop quizzes had been multiple choice. But this test was different. These were essay questions. He was supposed to write the answers in the blue booklet. Glancing over the questions, he felt confident that he knew the answers. Now, if he could just find the right words. He slowly and carefully began to write.

Raja was so intent on what he was writing that he was startled to hear Miss Brown say, "Time's up."

"But I'm not finished. I still have two questions to go!" exclaimed Raja.

"You will have to stop anyway. Hand in what you have finished," instructed his teacher.

Reluctantly, Raja handed in his paper. He felt like a sleepwalker the rest of the day. That evening at home, he studied for his algebra and biology tests and tried to put the American history exam out of his mind. In his dreams that night, little blue test booklets floated around him in a dark hallway. Gaunt cows stumbled toward him, their pale eyes reflected in the shiny linoleum floors. As they chased him down the hall, they swallowed the booklets and growled at him.

When Miss Brown handed out their test booklets at the end of class the following morning, Raja turned the cover just enough to see the grade she had marked in the top right corner.

The world seemed to move in slow circles around him. It can't be, he thought. I knew the answers. This mark can't be correct. The bell rang. He shoved the test booklet into his backpack and ran blindly from the room, forgetting to rise with the others and say "Good bye, Madam."

Steve rushed after him, snagging him by the sleeve.

"Raja! What's wrong?" he said in alarm, pushing Raja against the wall and bracing him.

Raja felt like a wild man, out of control. There were spots in front of his eyes and he was having trouble breathing. "I didn't get a top grade, Steve. I have failed. I have failed. What will I do now?"

Steve tried to calm him. "Easy, buddy. I know you did your best. Top scores are important in my country too. You haven't failed, OK? This is just a temporary setback. Now calm down and let's get you to your other classes. You have tests in biology and algebra today, right? You absolutely cannot let this distract you, you got that? Raja, are you listening to me? You got that?"

Raja took a minute to filter everything Steve was saying to him. "Yes, Steve, I've got that," he said solemnly. He might have failed, but he could still "go out swinging," as the Americans put it. He punched Steve in the arm and managed a smile. "I didn't mean to zone out on you, Steve. I apologize."

Steve slung an arm around Raja's shoulder and walked with him up the stairs. "Zone out, Raja? Good one! Do you have that one in your American expression copybook?"

Raja put the history exam out of his mind and focused on his two other exams. He also had a business exam the next day and an English exam the day after that. Still, his disappointment loomed like dark cumulus clouds piling up in the sky.

Steve met Raja as he left the building at the end of the day. They walked silently side by side. Mitsuko was waiting for them at the door. She could see that Raja was upset.

"Come over here and sit down, Raja. You, too, Steve. Now tell me, what's wrong?"

Raja took the booklet out of his backpack and handed it to Mitsuko.

Then it was as if all his emotions and fears just tumbled out. He knew he wasn't making any sense and he knew his words were all mixed up and that he was pronouncing everything wrong, but he was unable to stop himself.

"You know how hard I am studying ven you helped me and I vas certain dat I could be getting a top score and I needing a top score and I am not getting it and my parents vill be so disappointed that I have failed because everything depends on dis one score and I knew the answers but couldn't be having time to finish and dere ver so many strange names and I am not being able to write fast enough and if I can't get into school in India I vill not be able to care for my parents and . . ."

"Whoa, Raja!" Mitsuko interrupted. "Let's talk about this. First and most important, everything does not depend on this one exam score. Where did you get that idea?"

A look of comprehension slowly crawled across Steve's face. He glanced at Mitsuko as if to say, so that's what this is all about?

"That is the way it is in India," Raja explained breathlessly. "Ve haf to memorize and study much for the one grade that we get—"

"OK, Raja. Stop." Mitsuko raised her hand in gentle warning. "Now listen to me. It is not like that here. Miss Brown will average all of the grades you have made in her class. All of the essays, the pop quizzes, your reports, your attendance, your behavior, the way you answer questions in class discussions, AND your exams—all of those will be averaged together for your final grade. One bad grade does not mean you will fail the course. As a matter of fact, you've had such good grades so far that I bet you could fail your final exam and still not fail this class. Not that I'm advising you to do that, you understand."

Raja looked from Mitsuko to Steve to Mitsuko again. Could this be true? He felt a lump in his throat and he squeezed his eyes hard to keep from crying. He did not want his friends to see him cry. But they had already pulled him to his feet and wrapped their arms around him.

That night as Dad and Mitsuko walked up the stairs and past Raja's room, they could hear him inside reciting.

"This, that, these, those, them, there, thus, thing, therapy, theater, thanks, through, throttle, throw, thumb, three, thoroughbred, thorn, thrifty . . ."

Dad looked down at Mitsuko with a quizzical expression. Mitsuko shrugged and raised her hands in a helpless gesture.

"I just live here, Dad. Face it, we're a weird family. It's bound to rub off on Raja."

Letters Home

Dear Father, Mother and sisters,

Since I last wrote you, it has snowed many times here. I had heard about snow and seen pictures in books, but pictures do not do justice to such a beautiful thing. My dear sisters, Devika and Runa, you would have such fun in the snow! Steve and Mitsuko and I built a snowman last week. Then Mom Jade decided that our snowman was too lonely and she came out with us and helped to build a wife and child for our snowman. They have colorful hats and scarves, carrots for noses, and radishes for eyes and mouths. I was told that some people use pieces of coal for the nose and mouth, but we did not have any coal and so Mom Jade thought radishes would work. While we were working on the snow family, Brad sneaked up and starting throwing snowballs at us. This is called a snow fight. You pat snow until it is the size of baseballs and throw these at one another. It is not a battle, but a game. It was great fun! Yesterday we started to build a snow fort. We have maybe three feet of snow on the ground now. It covers everything like one of Mother's lovely white saris.

I am also making extra money shoveling the snow from some of the driveways. These are the people whose lawns I mowed earlier in the fall. A few more people have asked us to do this and so Brad and Steve and I keep very busy. It is a good workout for me and the money I have earned has enabled me to mail the Christmas gifts you will be receiving soon. I hope you like what I have picked out for you.

In your last letter, Father, you mentioned that your university will be getting computers soon. If you are able to access the Internet, then we can write e-mails to one another and we will receive our e-mails on the same day they are sent! And not only that, the same hour they are sent! Isn't that a wonderful thing? I will be taking a computer course after Christmas, when the new semester begins, so I hope to learn much more about this. All of my other classes will remain the same.

My American family is very good to me, but I miss you so much. Especially now when the Christmas lights remind me that in India you are preparing for Christmas too. I will miss decorating the tree with you this year. Thank you, Mother, for sending the angel ornament

*with me. I was surprised to find it in my
luggage but now I know why you tucked it
away for me. When I hang it on the Jade's
tree, I will be thinking of you. May God keep
you safe until I return to you in June.*

Your loving son and brother, Raja

"I'm sorry, kids," Dad Jade said. "I need the car
tonight for a meeting. Can't you catch a ride with
someone else?"

"What if I take you to your meeting, honey, and
then drive the kids to the game?" Mom suggested.
"After all, Brad, Phil and Steve are all playing tonight,
and we've already missed so many of their away
games."

"So, you'd take them over, then come back for me,
then go back over? Darling, that's a 45-minute drive
over and then back again. And you'd miss most of the
game anyway."

"I think we need another car," Mom said
at last.

"Well, we do own a car dealership, you know." Dad
scratched his head, then looked up at Mitsuko and Raja.
"Having one car hasn't been much of a problem
because Mom and I go to work together. Still, what we
really need is another licensed driver."

Mitsuko was nudging Raja's foot under the table and
Raja was trying very hard not to crack a smile.

"Well, Brad is taking Driver's Ed next summer, isn't
he?" Mom asked.

"But that doesn't solve our problem right now. We are in so many activities at school and church and sometimes I can't tell if I'm coming or going," Dad said, sighing. Then he looked at Raja, as if seeing him for the first time.

"Raja, how would you like to learn to drive?"

The swift kick he felt against his leg told him he better say yes. But before he could answer, Mom was talking again.

"Oh, honey, I don't know about that. It's winter, the roads are icy, and Raja is not used to American ways. I mean, they even drive on the other side of the road over there." Mom looked almost tragic in her worry.

But there was a determined glint in Dad's eyes. "Which is an excellent point, my dear. If you recall, I've driven in India. Anyone that can survive traffic over there can handle the worst America has to offer!"

At that, Raja finally allowed himself to laugh.

The problem that night was solved when Dad called around and found someone willing to pick him up for the meeting. Mom drove Raja and Mitsuko to the game and stayed with them. Later she told Dad that if she hadn't been able to stay, she would have missed Brad's three-point shot at the half-time buzzer.

Dad set aside the next Saturday for Raja's first driving lesson. It was already getting dark after school by now, and Dad wanted to work with Raja during daylight hours at first. As Raja waited excitedly for Saturday to arrive, the hours and days seemed to move like an ox-drawn cart on a superhighway full of speeding racecars! During every free moment he could manage, Raja read the driver's manual Dad had given him.   Walking to and from school, he studied the shapes and colors of road signs and memorized what they represented. He watched the traffic rushing by him on busy streets and looked for things drivers were doing right and wrong. He sat in the station wagon in the garage and familiarized himself with the gauges and pedals and steering column. He even looked under the hood and tried to understand how the engine worked.

Finally Saturday arrived and he and Dad were off. Dad selected a parking lot outside a factory at the edge of town. No one was working that weekend, so they had the entire parking lot to themselves. The snow had been cleared earlier and the asphalt was open and relatively clear of ice and packed snow.

"Raja," Dad began, "the most important thing I can tell you today is that you must always be in control when you drive a car.   All your attention must be focused on what you are doing, on the decisions you must make, on the possible things that could happen. We call it driving defensively. I'm going to tell you something that might sound strange to you. Expect the other guy to make mistakes. Yes, that's what I said. Expect him to do the wrong thing. That means that you cannot trust the other driver to always do the right thing. For instance, other drivers may not give you the right of way. Other drivers may pass you illegally. Other drivers may tailgate, or run a red light, or dart out in front of you. Learn to drive in such a way that you

EXPECT these things to happen. Then you will be driving defensively and you will be prepared to react quickly when there is a problem."

Dad drove slowly around the parking lot, showing Raja how his legs and hands worked together. He drove forward, then in reverse. He explained the proper way to place one's hands on the steering wheel, how to use the turn signals and headlights.

Then it was Raja's turn. Raja had watched Dad a hundred times when he was driving, but had never paid attention to the details. Now he listened carefully as Dad showed him how to adjust the mirrors and seat to his own size. Raja's legs were longer than Dad's, so the seat had to be pushed back further. Raja was taller, so the mirrors had to be set at a different angle. They buckled their seatbelts. Dad let Raja start the car and put it in "drive," then told him to gently press down on the accelerator to prevent the car from lurching forward. When Raja braked, he learned not to hit the brake pedal too hard. They drove around and around the parking lot, stopping and starting, driving in reverse.

Dad even directed him toward an icy patch and asked Raja to brake hard. As the car began to slide, Dad explained how Raja could "correct" the slide and regain control.

After the lesson, Dad drove to a convenience store and they bought a couple of drinks—coffee for Dad and hot cocoa for Raja. Sitting in the car and sipping their drinks, Dad asked Raja several questions from the driver's manual. Raja answered them all correctly.

"You've been doing your homework, Raja," Dad complimented him.

"But I have much to learn still," Raja replied. "Do you know what I used to think the *R* was for on the steering column? *RUN!*"

Dad chuckled. "So, did you think *D* meant *DASH*?"

"And maybe the *N* could be for *NERVOUS*, for how Mom feels about me driving!" Raja joked.

"As long as you don't think *P* is for *PANIC* when you take your driver's test!"

They laughed a long time over that. Finally Dad was serious again.

"Raja, tell me some of the things that can distract a driver while he is driving."

Raja thought about this for a few moments. "I have seen sometimes when someone is talking on a phone in the car and they are not paying attention."

"Very good. What else?"

"A pretty girl walking on the street might be a distraction."

"Ah, Raja! Yes, that too. Or getting interested in something you see while you are driving. I always seem to get distracted when I see tractors in the field! Mom tells me to pay attention or I will cause a wreck!"

Raja smiled. "I am noticing, ah, I have noticed that it is easy to lose attention when you, how you say, fiddle with the music?"

"That's right. Sometimes we let little things divert our attention. Playing with the radio dial, or changing CDs, even adjusting the heater. The same thing can happen when you have several people in the car and they're all talking and laughing and having a good time. It is very hard for the driver to stay focused — but that is EXACTLY when you must be your most alert."

Raja nodded thoughtfully and looked over at Mr. Jade. "Dad, I understand what you are saying. Mitsuko and Steve and Brad are very special to me. I will drive defensively. I will drive always as if Jesus is sitting with us."

Mr. Jade tilted his head slightly and smiled. "Well, now, that just about says it all, doesn't it?"

Over the next few weeks, Dad and Raja moved from the parking lot to little-traveled country roads and then to the neighborhood streets and some of the less congested streets of the town. By then, Raja had a learner's permit. When Dad was satisfied that he was able to handle himself in tough, winter conditions, he encouraged Raja to drive on busy city streets and eventually the highway.

Shortly before Christmas, on a cold, snowy day, Raja and Dad arrived at the license bureau for his appointment. Raja first took his written test and had his eyes checked.

"How are you feeling, Raja?" Dad asked him as they waited for Raja's name to be called.

"A little scared," Raja confided, flipping anxiously through the driver's manual.

"That's OK. That will keep you cautious. But notch it down a little. You know, keep it at N and not P, you got that?"

Raja laughed. "Yes, Dad, I've got that!"

Then his name was called and he rose to face the officer who was approaching them. "Raja Shah? I'm Officer Sanchez. Looks like you aced your written test, young man. Now let's see how you do on the road."

When Raja's car slid into the car behind him, nudging the bumper as he pulled out of the parking space, he figured he'd blown the test right then. But Officer Sanchez told him to continue.

It seemed that everything that could possibly happen, did. Someone ran a red light and nearly hit him, but Raja managed to stop in time. Officer Sanchez radioed in the other vehicle's license number and called for another unit to pursue the offender. Meanwhile, Raja was watching in the rearview mirror as the car behind him approached too fast and began to slide. Fortunately, Raja was able to pull into a driveway out of the way of the fishtailing vehicle. Then, when he was asked to parallel park, the station wagon got stuck. Raja remembered what Dad had taught him and "rocked" the car, using "Drive" and "Reverse" until he wriggled the car free.

When they finally arrived back at the license bureau, Officer Sanchez smiled broadly and slapped him on the shoulder. "I don't know about you, son, but I'm sure glad that's over!"

Raja didn't exactly consider that a compliment, but apparently it was good enough to earn him an American driver's license!

Dear Father, Mother and sisters,

We are in the middle of the American winter break which they call Christmas vacation. By now you have received the presents I sent you. I hope they arrived on time. When you have a computer and are able to e-mail messages, you will learn that the way I sent the packages is sometimes called "snail mail." That is a funny expression! I hope that you like the can of cocoa I sent. I think that is my favorite American food. Mrs. Jade wrote instructions for you to follow on how to make it. Don't forget to put in the marshmallows. Devika and Runa especially will like those, I am sure! I also hope Devika and Runa like the beanie bag babies. Mitsuko picked them out and assured me that these are "hot" American collectibles. She also assisted me in selecting the wallet for you, Father, and the handbag for you, Mother.

It is a very quiet time here, this winter break. Our exams are over and we are in between semesters. I am reading a lot and practicing my English. I am also still shoveling snow. We do not seem to run out of that here! Yesterday we took down the big Christmas tree that was in the family room. Brad and I took it into the backyard and tied it to one of the clothesline poles. Some people burn their trees or throw them away, but the Jade family puts seed bells and strings of popcorn on the tree for the birds. It is almost as pretty now in the backyard as it was in the family room.

Christmas Day was very nice. We attended a special service at our church and then came home and opened presents. Mr. and Mrs. Jade gave me two very nice sweaters and leather driving gloves. Brad gave me some jumper cables to keep in the car I am driving. Mitsuko gave me a little goose figurine with a sock hat and scarf. Steve surprised me with a New York Yankees baseball hat! This is funny because my present to him was a New York Knicks hat and both hats are almost the same color. Mrs. Jade liked the little crystal bell I gave her. She said she will add it to her collection which she keeps in a special cabinet in the living room. Mr. Jade said the bookends were just what he needed for his office. Thank you, Mother, for suggesting that, as well as the lace table scarf for Mitsuko's dresser. Brad also likes the poster of Pelé I found in an old bookstore. It took me a while to find that, but it was worth it to hear him yell "Yes!" I think I told you that he is a soccer fan—and a good player, too.

As I mentioned, I am driving now. Mr. Jade brought home a car for us to use. It is not my car but I am permitted to drive it while I am in America. Brad calls it a "tank," and says it wouldn't break his heart if I took it back to

India. He will get his license in the summer and it will be his car to drive then. Mr. Jade says he likes that this car has a box shape and a long hood and trunk to better protect the driver and people in it. I am glad to have learned to drive while I am here and Mr. Jade says it helps the family out with our busy schedules. I have been told that I am a good driver, although Mitsuko says I drive like an old lady. Mr. Jade says better that than a jackrabbit. He says too many young people drive with a "lead foot." I will have to find out what that means.

In my next letter, I will tell you how my new semester is going. As I said, I will only have one new course, the computer class, but I will have a couple of new teachers. Please pray that I will keep good grades and make you proud of me. I remember you in my prayers every morning and every night. And that is not the only time I think of you. May God keep you safe until I see you again in June.

Your loving son and brother, Raja

Home Cooking

Raja had had more than enough of winter. Made more tedious by cold, harsh days and long, dark nights, January had stretched on as if it would never end. Now it was the middle of February and more winter loomed before them. Each morning they got up in the dark and each afternoon they went home in the dark. Three of Raja's classrooms had no windows and Raja sometimes felt as if the walls were closing in on him. His new Biology II teacher was more demanding than the first one had been and required more written reports. His English teacher had assigned a term paper and to make certain his students wouldn't write this at the last minute, he insisted they turn in an outline, note cards and rough drafts of what they had written each week.

In order to keep up, Raja found himself working on homework until late every night, as well as most Saturdays and Sunday afternoons. There was very little time for anything else. He had even stopped going to basketball games. One Tuesday evening, Mitsuko pleaded with him to take her to an away game.

"Ask Mom or Dad, Mitsuko," he snapped. "I just

can't take time to drive you tonight. I have too much homework." When he looked up from his books, she was heading out his door, but not before he saw the hurt on her face. He got up quickly and followed her into the hallway.

"I am sorry, Mitsuko," he said.

Her angry, hurt voice trailed behind her as she ran down the stairs. "If you had taken time to notice, Raja, Mom and Dad are at the church board meeting tonight. And you're not the only one with homework, buster. I have to work twice as hard because I help you so much. I just got done, as a matter of fact. But it's so late that all my other friends have already left for the game."

Raja caught up with her by the time she reached the kitchen. He placed a hand on her shoulder.

"Then I will take you, Mitsuko," he said apologetically.

"No, never mind. It's no big deal. We'll be late anyway."

He grabbed their jackets and unhooked the car keys from the key rack by the door.

"You are right, Mitsuko. I have been having my head in the dirt—"

"Sand," she corrected, pretending to study something on the wall behind him.

"Yes, sand. I have been, how you say, all wrapped up on myself."

"In myself." Her arms were folded across her chest and she was tapping one foot impatiently.

"Wrapped up in myself. That is right. And maybe

it would be good to get out of the house and have some fun tonight. I owe you least much for helping me.

"At least that much," she corrected again. She was looking down at her feet now, chewing on her lower lip. Apparently she was waiting for something else. American girls were great mysteries and this one standing in front of him was the greatest mystery of all.

"And I am very, very sorry for hurting your feelings by what I said," he ventured. "I am not mad at you, Mitsuko. Will you forgive me?"

Finally she looked up at him and smiled. "You get the car warmed up, Raja, and I'll leave Mom and Dad a note, OK?"

They arrived during half time and worked their way through the crowd to the refreshment stand. While Raja was ordering hotdogs and drinks, four of Mitsuko's girlfriends spotted them and rushed over. Raja cringed when he saw that giggling Sierra was among them. He tried to pretend he didn't see them coming by counting out the money he needed to pay for their snacks.

"There you are, Mitsuko. We wondered what was taking you so long," one girl said.

"But we can see why, with such a cute boyfriend as Raja," another one said before the first girl had finished speaking.

"Sometime you should invite us to double-date with you," a third girl joined in. Mitsuko flushed bright red and held up her hands.

"Whoa, kids," she said and her voice cracked with

forced humor. "First thing, Raja is NOT my boyfriend, OK?"

Two of the girls rolled their eyes.

"Then why do you keep him all to yourself?" Sierra crooned.

"Second, we are NOT on a date," Mitsuko continued, ignoring Sierra. "I'm not allowed to date yet. And Raja isn't allowed to date at all. Right?" she said, elbowing him sharply. He nearly spilled one of the drinks. "You can jump in here any time, Raja," she muttered.

"Ah, yes," he said, finally catching on. "Mitsuko is right. My parents would not permit me to date. It is not the Indian way of doing things."

"Raja, in case you haven't noticed, you're not in India," Sierra said, batting her eyes and flipping her hair over her shoulder. "If Mitsuko doesn't want to date you, I'd be happy to. Your parents would never have to know."

Raja gulped hard. All of these girls were looking at him with sharp, curious eyes. Mitsuko also had a strange look in her eyes, as if she was waiting to see how he would respond to this challenge. But even though Raja was shocked and embarrassed by what Sierra had just said, he had no doubt about what was in his heart.

"You do not seem to understand, Sierra," he said, surprised at how calm and authoritative his voice sounded. "God would know if I disobeyed my parents. I would not dishonor Him or them in that way."

Then he nodded his head slightly at Mitsuko. "Mitsuko, if you can manage the hotdogs, I will carry the drinks."

As they threaded their way to the bleachers, he thought how odd it was that the shock he had felt was now registered on the faces of those four girls! But Mitsuko's pixie face, framed by her beautiful, shining black hair, was glowing with something like pride or awe or maybe something else he couldn't define. It didn't matter. Sitting next to her on the bleachers, he realized that he was exactly where he wanted to be— even if it wasn't called a date.

By Thursday, Raja had long forgotten Tuesday's game. His homework seemed to be piling up like the snowdrifts all over the neighborhood. And tomorrow he had a biology test.

Steve had stayed for basketball practice. Usually Raja remained and watched, but today he only stayed an hour, then decided to walk home alone. It was nearly dark. The last red glow of the setting sun filtered through the leafless branches of the trees and threw shadows across the glistening snow. The shadows looked like prison bars to Raja. He suddenly felt very lonely and far away from home.

Then as he entered the Jade kitchen, he caught the scent of something familiar.

"Are you cooking something just for me, Mom?" he asked, as he shrugged off his backpack and coat. "It smells like India when my mother cooks curried chicken."

Mom Jade looked up and smiled. "Well, no. Actually, Raja, I was going to prepare stir-fry chicken, as I've done before. I think right now you must be smelling the onions," she explained.

"Do you suppose that I could cook some Indian food sometime? My mother sent some spices with me. I have them upstairs in a box. I did not think of using them until just now."

Mom studied him for a minute, then turned the burner off. "How's your schedule tonight?" she asked. "No, wait, don't answer that. I KNOW your schedule!"

They both laughed. Then Mom said, "OK, Raja, we've got to eat, and you always study after we eat anyway, so let's go for it. What do you need?"

He frowned and went through a mental list. "Let's see, a large pan or the wok would work. And oil, the kind for high temperatures."

"Peanut oil," Mom said, her voice muffled as she bent over to reach into one of the lower cabinets.

"And chicken."

"I've already got that out."

"Good, good, and onions. More than you have in that pan. Lots of onions! And garlic, a bunch of that. Oh, Mom, I have seen my mother cook many times but I have never cooked before and I am having trouble remembering all the things I need."

"That's OK, we'll make it up as we go along! I have a basic idea of what we might need. Why don't you run up and change and bring down your spices and I'll gather a few other things we might want."

When Raja came back into the kitchen, Mom tied an apron around him. She picked the white chef's apron Dad Jade wore sometimes when he barbecued, instead of the ruffled calico print she frequently wore.

Raja was already crushing the garlic with the side of the French knife and then mincing it. Mom was impressed. Apparently Raja had paid more attention to his mother's techniques than he realized. He placed Mom Jade's big wok on the burner and turned the heat on high. Next, he poured about a cup of oil in the pan. When the oil began to smoke, he put in the garlic, ginger, and curry powder. The spices crackled and popped in the hot oil while he chopped up two large onions.

Mom was a little worried. "You might want to turn the heat down, Raja. You will burn your spices."

"No," Raja assured her, "the oil is supposed to be this hot."

When he added the onions, however, he realized that Mom was right. The spices were beginning to turn black. He quickly turned the heat down because he did not want to burn the onions too.

As Raja stirred the onions until they were golden brown, he asked, "Mom, I will need to add the chicken soon."

"Why don't I cut that up for you?" she offered quickly. She noticed that while Raja had chopped onions, pieces had flown everywhere. She wasn't exactly looking forward to cleaning pieces of raw chicken off the walls and floor too.

The hot oil splattered and sputtered as Raja dropped the pieces of chicken into the pan.

"Be careful, Raja, that the grease does not splatter on the kitchen carpet. Cover the pan with the lid when you put the chicken in," Mom suggested.

Raja didn't remember his mother ever covering her curried chicken while it cooked. But then, they did not have carpet on their kitchen floor either. He smiled at Mom Jade as he placed the lid over the wok.

"Should I turn down the fire now that the lid is on?" he asked.

"Good thinking, Raja. You're right. The heat will build up. After a while, everything will settle down a little and you can take the lid off.

Raja suddenly had an idea. He was having such fun that he wanted to share it with his best friends. "Mom, I think Steve is home from practice by now. Can I call him and invite him over? Maybe he could bring some Ugandan food?"

"Why not?" Mom answered. She hadn't seen Raja this happy in a long time.

Raja hurried to telephone Steve while Mom watched the chicken. This was going to be fun! Curious about the interesting smells drifting through the house, Mitsuko had wandered into the kitchen When Raja hung up the phone and turned to her. "Mitsuko, I am cooking Indian tonight. Steve is coming over in a little while with something Ugandan. Would you like to cook something Japanese?"

Then he whipped around and looked at Mom. "If

that is all right with you, Mom?" he asked hesitantly.

But Mitsuko had already barreled past him and was digging around in a cabinet for a saucepan.

"So now this is turning into an international meal!" Mom said, chuckling. "OK, Raja what else do you need? What can I do for you?"

Raja frowned slightly as he tried to concentrate. Mitsuko was not making it easy for him, as she was rushing around the kitchen, opening and closing drawers and cabinets.

"Your wok takes up too much room, Raja!" she complained, bumping into him as she tried to fit her saucepan on the burner next to Raja's.

"Honey," Mom said calmly, "why don't you move that to the back left burner. Yes, that's good. See, you have more room to work."

"Why isn't this chicken done yet, Mom?" Raja interrupted. He was jabbing it with a fork.

"You have to remember that meat takes longer to cook, Raja. Raise the heat a bit, that's it."

By then Steve had arrived with his Ugandan beef broccoli dish. "This will need to bake in the oven," he explained to Mrs. Jade. She set the thermostat and timer on the oven and put Steve's casserole dish inside. She was also thinking she needed another arm or two, or at least a referee's cap!

When the chicken was finally tender, Raja said, "There's too much juice on the chicken. We will need to let it cook down." Then his eyes got wide. "Chappaties!" he suddenly yelped. "I need chappaties!"

Mom turned from Mitsuko to Raja again. "OK, Raja, I give up. What's a chappatie?"

Raja tried to explain. "I must have some flour and water, and that thing you use to make them flat and round." He made gestures with his hands.

Mom laughed as she took the rolling pin from the drawer and waved it in the air. "Is this what you're talking about, the rolling pin?"

"Ah, yes, exactly so! I will make them if you watch the chicken."

Steve had already moved in next to Raja, who was wrestling with the rolling pin. Mitsuko was preparing Japanese fried rice and was now bumping elbows with Mom Jade.

Mom glanced behind her at the cloud of flour and flurry that used to be Raja Shah. She was glad he was wearing an apron, because he had flour all over it, on his shirt sleeves, and even on his face. She spotted Brad peeking around the corner and was going to enlist his help, but he ducked out of the way just in time.

"They just won't get round, Mom," Raja said mournfully. He was pressing and pushing as if he were laying pavement with a steamroller. "It looked so easy when my mother made them!"

Everyone laughed as he held up a piece of dough and said, "See? It looks like a pair of pants, but it is supposed to be round!"

Steve took the rolling pin and said, "Let me try. I know how to make these." After he added a little more flour, he worked them into very presentable circles.

"Now we have to fry them in the oil." More bustling and clanking of dishes and pans as he found a dish and scooped up the curried chicken and vegetables from the wok. Raja then heated up the oil again and carefully added the chappaties one at a time to fry them. Steve found another dish to put them on as Raja dipped the finished chappaties out of the sizzling oil.

Things were progressing well until Raja's eyes got round again.

"Rice!" he yelped. "We need rice!"

"But I'm making fried rice," Mitsuko reminded him.

"No, that is something completely different!" Raja was rocketing all over the kitchen, wild with excitement. Steve was bent over laughing.

"Oh, Raja," Mom said. "The kind of rice you are talking about will take another twenty minutes! We should have been cooking it on the back burner while we prepared these other dishes."

"I am sorry, Mom. But we must have it! How could I have forgotten such an important thing? I mean, before I came here, I ate rice every day!" He looked positively tragic.

Mom said in a soothing voice, "I'll hurry and make your rice for you. Your international dinner will not be ruined. You will just need to wait a little longer before you can eat."

"I love you, Mom," Raja said, kissing her on the cheek and leaving a smudge of flour on her face.

And so, nearly three hours after they had started, six hungry people sat around the big dining room table in the Jade house. Mom had finally snagged Brad long enough to get him to set the table and light the candles. Now they linked hands in the candlelight and thanked God for His provision. Outside the wind blew and sleet smacked against the windows, but inside the Jades' dining room the light was golden and the atmosphere was warm. And in no time at all, the food was completely gone! The international meal had been a great success.

"And just where do you think you are going?" Mom chided, as Raja, Mitsuko, Brad, and Steve headed upstairs after dinner.

"Mom, we have to study now," Raja answered. "I have a biology test tomorrow."

"I'm going to help him," Steve said.

"Latin homework," Mitsuko added.

"Uh, gotta read a chapter in government," Brad muttered.

"Nope," Mom declared. "About face, forward march. He that maketh mess, must clean up the mess. The law according to Mom Jade."

"Awwwwww, Mom!" came the chorus.

But as it turned out, unmaking the mess was nearly as much fun as making it. The friends laughed and clowned around and found that by working together, they were able to finish quickly.

Mom ran her finger over the counter when they were done. "OK, good job," she said, trying to act like a drill sergeant "You picked up all the grease. You put everything away. You are dismissed."

Unmaking the mess was nearly as much fun as making it.

Since it was late, Dad offered to drive Steve home.

"Thank you, Mom," Raja said before walking upstairs. "This has been a special night for me."

"We can do it again, Raja," she answered. "Perhaps next time on the weekend instead of a school night, though? It's so late now, are you sure you'll be able to study?"

"He'll be fine, Mom," Mitsuko teased. "That hot curry will keep his brain alert for some time tonight!"

Raja laughed too, but the evening of cooking had brought back memories of home and reminded him once again of his reason for coming to America. He was determined to study hard that night until he was certain he knew all the material for the test. He would not disappoint his parents.

The Boy in the Mirror

On a windy day in March, Raja paused outside the school office to brush the hair from his eyes. How changeable the weather was in America! It was always so hot and dry in India. Now Raja would be experiencing a new season in America — spring. He had gone through autumn and winter. He realized with a sudden pang, that he would not experience summer here. In fact, according to the terms of the exchange program, he would have to leave the day after graduation. There had been some trouble initially in getting the paperwork through for his visa. By the time the authorities had straightened everything out, he had lost three months. Still, it was more than the majority of people in India would ever have.

His attention was suddenly drawn to a notice on the bulletin board outside the office. *ATTENTION! Math Student Needs Tutor. Call if interested.*

He started to walk away. He would not have time

to even consider this. Then he remembered a conversation he'd had with Phil shortly after he had arrived in America. Phil had asked him about the notebooks he carried.

"This is one of my copybooks," Raja had answered. "I try taking notes on everything the teachers say. Then when I am studying for the exams I am having good study notes to remember me by."

"I don't worry about taking notes," Phil had said. "I just try to remember in my head. It's no big deal if I don't get an 'A'. I'll be satisfied with a 'C'. I'm not going to college anyway, so why should I worry about it?"

"That is not good enough for me," said Raja. "I have to do a lot of studying and memorizing because your words are sounding so different from mine. My dad is a professor in a college in India and students often coming to him for 'too-shun' after class hours."

Phil chuckled, "I wish I had half your brains, Raja. I bet you could give me 'too-shun,' even if your English sounds funny. If I wanted 'too-shun,' that is."

"But, Phil, you are very good in basketball. In college you could play but you will be needing scholarship and for that you will have to be having good grades."

"Nope, not interested, pal. Sounds like work to me."

"Yes, it is. It is important for me to get good grades so that I can go home and take care of my parents in their old age."

Raja now shifted the heavy backpack across his shoulders as he stood outside the school office. Of course, he didn't have time to consider tutoring a student in math. He had to make the most of his remaining time. And Raja Shah could not take his good grades for granted. He earned every one of them with hard, concentrated effort.

Still, something nagged him. Mitsuko had been generous enough with her time to tutor him. What would he have done without her? And, after all, he was good in math. He had an 'A' average.

Raja thought about this all day and even prayed about it during study hall. When he left for home that afternoon, he stopped by the office and copied down the phone number of the boy named Harry who wanted "too-shun." He wasn't shoveling snow these days and it would be a while before the mowing season began. Raja thought this might be a good way to earn some money to buy some parting gifts for his family. As an afterthought, he scribbled a note to himself in one of his copybooks. He had to remember to write his mother. He thought perhaps he would give his host family some Indian gifts and he needed to give his mother time to mail them to him.

Harry seemed surprised when he met Raja for the first tutoring session the following Wednesday evening. They had decided to meet on Mondays and Wednesdays at 7 o'clock in the school library. But after their first session together, Harry felt comfortable with Raja. Raja was patient, understanding, and didn't make fun of Harry's inability to grasp certain concepts. And he was creative, too, sometimes making Harry laugh just when he thought he might cry from frustration. Three weeks later, Harry rushed into the library with a huge smile on his face. He was waving a math test paper. Raja realized at that moment that he was getting as much out of giving "too-shun" as Harry was.

The weeks began to gain momentum as spring unfurled around them. It seemed Raja would wake on Monday morning and before he knew it, it was Friday. Soon it seemed he was in a blur of tests and papers and reports and biology lab tests and the "monster term paper," as Mitsuko termed it. She had been a close ally throughout the semester, especially as they entered the final six weeks. Each night when Raja was not tutoring, she and Raja could be found at the dining room table bent over their books. Sometimes their heads rested against one another as Mitsuko carefully checked Raja's papers. Once when Steve was working with them, Mitsuko got up to sharpen her pencil in the kitchen. Raja's head turned slowly as he watched her walk away.

"Someone's mind is not on term papers. Someone's mind is on Mitsuko," Steve whispered in a sing-song voice, then laughed when Raja glanced back at him and blushed furiously.

One night as Mitsuko flipped through one of his notebooks, she noticed that Raja had been keeping track of his grades throughout the semester. "Raja, are these all your grades so far?" she asked.

He nodded. "Yes, the ones I have been given, although not the ones for some things like answering in class and some reports I have not received back yet."

"Why don't we average these and see if we can estimate where you are, so we can see what you need to fine-tune?"

They worked a few minutes on separate scores, then combined their results.

Raja took one look and yelped, "Look, Mitsuko, I have a high B so far! All the hard work is paying off. And it is because of you!"

Mitsuko scrunched her nose as if it wasn't any big deal. "Hey, you know, Raja, actually you are doing me a favor."

"What's that?" he asked. What could he possibly have done for her except keep her from her own studies?

"Well, I'll have these courses down pat by the time I'm a senior! I bet I could test out and graduate ahead of everyone in my class!"

When Raja received his final grades, it was no surprise to anyone in the Jade household that he was graduating in the top ten percent of his class. Only Raja seemed astonished.

"Do you know that this one 'C' in my country would have been enough to keep me from graduating?" he said solemnly. "But here in America with the averaging of grades, I had enough 'A' grades to compensate."

Mitsuko was thinking at that moment how nice it was to hear Raja's flawless English and to know she had been a part of helping him learn to say words like "compensate."

Raja was thinking how proud his parents would be

and how he was not going to disappoint them after all. He had nearly completed his goal. With these top scores he would be able to attend college and find a good job. And with a good job, he would be able to help support his parents in their old age.

So why, at the very moment when he should be feeling so happy, was something pulling at his heart? He looked up and caught Mitsuko's dark, almond-shaped eyes gazing back at him. Was what he was feeling reflected in their stormy depths?

During lunch period on the last day of school, Raja took some time to walk across the school grounds where he had spent the last nine months. How different things looked to him now! What had frightened him at first was now familiar to him. He was able to converse comfortably in English and had made many good friends.

All at once, he felt as if he was being pulled in two different directions. He wanted to return to India and his family, to the bustling streets filled with motor bikes and rickshaws and rangy cows. But he didn't want to leave his American friends and family.

As he walked slowly into the lunchroom, some girls shouted, "Over here, Raja! We've saved a place for you!" He waved politely at them and turned to the serving table instead. On this last day of school, what else could they serve but hamburgers? Raja smiled broadly, remembering the emotions he had felt over that first ground beef patty, and how he had smothered it in applesauce. Holy cow, Steve had said. Raja assembled his hamburger, minus the applesauce, and turned toward the lunchroom again.

The girls who had invited him to eat with them were still waving him over, but only one girl interested him now. He gazed out over the tables until he spotted her to his left. She was smiling and pointing to a space next to her.

Sitting next to her, he suddenly realized that this would be their last school lunch together. Tomorrow was graduation day and the day after that he was scheduled to fly home to India. As students around him laughed and threw wadded paper napkins at one another, as the late May sun shone brightly through the windows high above them, it hit him with painful clarity. He might never see Mitsuko again.

Suddenly, Raja didn't feel hungry anymore. He pushed his French fries around on the plate with his fork.

"What's wrong, Raja?" Mitsuko asked. "You're not eating. That's not like you. You usually shovel it in like there's no tomorrow."

He looked at her and couldn't find the words to express what he was feeling. She placed a hand on his. "Raja, after school today, let's ride out to our oak tree, OK? I'm sure Mom will let us."

He nodded and tried to eat a French fry. It tasted like cardboard in his mouth.

They pedaled hard later that afternoon and reached the oak tree in record time. Collapsing under the tree, breathing hard from the exertion of their bicycle ride, it took them a few minutes to catch their breath.

It had been good to feel the rush of wind in his face again. Raja had not taken time to ride his bicycle this spring any farther than school and back. He would not be taking it back with him to India and had asked Dad to sell it for him. He would miss his beautiful blue and silver bike, but that is not what he would miss the most.

He and Mitsuko sat quietly for some time in the shade of the beautiful oak tree. There was so much to say, but he did not know where to start. At last, he simply reached across and took her hand in his.

"When I go back to India, I am going to miss you, Mitsuko" he said quietly. "You have helped me in so many ways and have become important in my life."

"I'll miss you too," she answered. Her voice was soft and gentle. He thought of the many sides of Mitsuko he had come to know over the last nine months—the funny Mitsuko, making faces at him over the table; the bossy Mitsuko, with her hands on her hips, tapping her foot in irritation; the beautiful Mitsuko, whose shiny black hair bounced around her when she raced down the stairs or whizzed by him on her bike; the kind Mitsuko, seeming to anticipate all of his feelings and fears.

"I wish we didn't have to part, but it is my duty to go back to India and care for my parents in their old age. I knew that before I came, but that doesn't make it any easier to tell you good-bye."

"Raja, perhaps you should know that I have asked my parents to consider letting me be an exchange student," she said, interrupting him. He turned and looked at her. "I mean, we always thought I would do this," she continued. "But we were thinking I would be an exchange student in my home country of Japan."

"And?" he pressed.

"And, well, I have asked them to see if I can be an exchange student in India instead."

Raja squeezed her hand. "This is wonderful news, Mitsuko!"

Before he could continue, she pressed a finger against his lips.

"Raja, I have only asked. It does not mean this will happen, you understand? If my parents say yes, there are still many details to be worked out. And India is a big country. I may not even be close to where you live." Her eyes were solemn and her chin trembled slightly.

He kissed the finger she had placed on his lips before answering her. "It does not matter, Mitsuko. India is not so big that I cannot find you!"

They rode home slowly. Once or twice they reached across and held hands, laughing as they tried to keep their bicycles balanced.

"We do this in India, Mitsuko!" he cried out. "When we are dodging rickshaws and sleeping cows, we hold hands!"

She laughed and he thought her laughter should always be a part of a sunny, spring afternoon—as important as the birds singing and the flowers blooming.

As they approached home, Mitsuko grew more

somber. "Raja, if it doesn't work out that I can come to India, will you write to me?"

"Of course I will write! And if I get a computer or have access to one at college, I will e-mail you!"

The sun shone brightly through his bedroom window when Raja awoke on graduation day. He immediately reached for his Hindi Bible and read a chapter, struggling to concentrate. Then he fell to his knees and prayed for his family in India and his family in America. He asked God to walk with him through the day and to keep his thoughts focused on the right things to do.

He wanted to look his best today, so he would wear the special suit his father had given him. Mom Jade must have pressed it for him, he noticed. And his best white shirt and the silk tie he saved for very special occasions. He saw that his Sunday shoes had been polished too. He must remember to thank her. After showering, shaving, and dressing, he took one last look in the mirror. The Raja he saw looking back at him was not the same boy who had looked at him with frightened eyes nine months ago. This Raja was now a young man and there was confidence shining in his face. He felt ready to face the world today.

He felt the same confidence and sense of joy as he walked across the platform to receive his diploma. His hopes and dreams and those of his parents culminated in this one moment.

"Raja Shah, graduating with honors," the principal announced.

Around him came the sound of cheers and applause. But Raja heard only one voice above the others. He remembered a certain basketball game on the day he had registered for school, and that same bright voice cheering him on from the bleachers.

"Go, Raja!"

"Alvida"

The afternoon turned into night and still people were coming and going at the Jade house. Raja's graduation reception was a complete surprise to him. How had Mom and Mitsuko hidden all of this from him? There were streamers, balloons, big cake, and presents. It seemed that everyone he had ever met in America was there! The pastor of the church was now finally leaving. Raja remembered how out of place he had felt the first time he attended church. Now the house was bustling with members and their children, all smiling and wishing him well.

However, all the cake and ice cream or the good wishes of his friends could not erase the ache in his heart. All of this only meant that tomorrow he would be leaving America. Still, he smiled and shook hands and thanked people warmly. Sometimes when he glanced around, he caught Mitsuko looking away suddenly, as if she had been watching him.

Late that night when everyone was gone, Mom chased Mitsuko and Raja out of the kitchen. "I can clean this up, you two," she said. "Why don't you take the last of that punch and go sit out on the porch for a while. It's a beautiful night."

They sat quietly in the porch swing and sipped their punch. When their glasses were empty, Raja placed them on the floor and then began rocking the swing gently back and forth. His long legs scraped the floor and he chuckled as he lifted them once in a while and let them stick straight out in front of him.

Finally he took a deep breath. "Mitsuko, you might not like India. Many of the things that you have become accustomed to here in America, you will not find in my homeland."

"True," she answered simply. "Guess I won't know if I like it or not unless I try, though."

He chuckled. Ah, Mitsuko, she was always so candid.

"And there might be some cultural misunderstandings, you understand?" he continued. "Many families will not allow a boy like me and a girl like you to be, ah, friends."

"What about YOUR family?" she asked.

"I don't know, Mitsuko. I have not talked to my parents about this. But we are Christians. We do not follow all of the cultural norms the others follow."

"Guess we'll just have to wait and see, huh?" she said, leaning her head against his shoulder. He put an arm around her and then pointed to the millions of twinkling stars in the night sky.

"Those stars are very far away from us and that is how I will feel about you when I am in India, that you are so very far away," he said, and his voice cracked.

"But, Raja, think of this. Each night when we look up, we will see the same stars above us. They will remind us that the same God who looks down on India is looking down on America."

Raja remembered thinking that very thing when he prayed by his bed on his first night in America."

"These stars will also remind us of each other," Mitsuko continued. "I will look up and it will be daytime where you are and I will think of you at college or dodging cows in the streets."

"Each night when we look up, we will see the same stars above us."

"And when I look up, it will be daytime here, and I will think of you riding your bike with the pink streamers and ringing that silly bell," he whispered, trying to sound cheerful.

"Hey, not for long, buster!" she quipped. "Before long, I'm driving the tank—if Brad doesn't wreck it first."

They both laughed and rocked gently in the porch swing.

"I have a gift for you, Mitsuko. Something I asked my mother to send."

"Ah, that must have been the package you got a couple of weeks ago. I wondered why you didn't tell us what was in it!"

Her eyes were curious and bright and for a while, at least, she seemed to forget the sadness that loomed ahead. She was already out of the swing and at the door.

"Well?" she said impatiently. "Are your going to show it to me or not?"

Upstairs in his room, his suitcases were scattered on the bed and floor. Dresser drawers were open and clothes hung out. Books, satchels, and boxes seemed to be everywhere.

"Good grief, Raja!" Mitsuko cried. "You haven't finished packing yet? What would you do without me?" She was already on her knees gathering up his belongings.

Raja joined her, but he was thinking, you are right, Mitsuko. What will I do without you?

It was nearly two o'clock in the morning before they

finished. Mom and Dad passed by the open door and wished them good night, urging them to finish and get some sleep.

As Mitsuko was leaving Raja's room, he caught her by the arm and handed her a colorfully wrapped box. She sat down at his desk and held it in her lap for a minute.

"Raja, the wrappings are so beautiful. I think that this is perfect just the way it is. I don't even have to open it!"

"But you must," he insisted. She carefully peeled away the Indian paper and silk ribbon. As she pulled off the lid, she gasped. She'd never seen a doll like this one. The little Indian doll was about ten inches tall, dressed in a teal green sari with golden trim. Her little arms held several golden bracelets, and she was wearing a necklace and earrings of gold. A red dot adorned her forehead. Mitsuko knew this meant the doll represented a married woman. For once, she was speechless.

"It is a Gujarati bridal doll in bridal costume," he said. "Do you like it?"

She touched the cool silk of the sari and whispered, "It is the most beautiful thing I have ever seen." A single tear fell and stained the bright green material.

Raja pulled her to her feet and hugged her, then released her. As she walked out his door, clutching the doll to her chest, he saw that there was no bounce in her step as before. He knew she was having as hard a time as he was.

Sleep eluded him as he tossed and turned on the

bed. So many thoughts tumbled over and over in his mind.

If he stayed in America and worked, Mitsuko and he could see each other. Was he foolish to go back to India where his future was limited and where there were few modern conveniences? Perhaps he could stay here and eventually bring his family over. Even as he thought it, he knew his family would not want to leave India.

Then he wondered, if Mitsuko comes over instead, she just might adjust nicely to Indian culture and his family might very well accept her with open arms. It could happen. But what if it didn't?

Still, at the back of all his tumbling thoughts was the reality of his original goal. He came to America for one reason, to learn what he needed to learn in order to return to India and take the firstborn son's place of responsibility. He continued to wrestle with the two pathways before him—whether to stay in America or return to India.

Finally, he crawled out of bed and fell to his knees. "Please, God," he pleaded. "Make me strong in the right decision."

And in that moment of pain and confusion, God spoke to him. Not audibly, but with a sense of calm settling over him like a warm blanket. Without any doubt, he knew that the right thing, the thing God wanted him to do, was to return to India. As for the rest? Well, that was something God would work out.

In the morning, Mom called to him, "Raja, it's time

to get up." But he was already awake and dressed. He had not been able to sleep a wink. He carried his bags and suitcases down the stairs and lined them up by the door. Then he sat down to eat his last breakfast with his American family.

They were a somber group this morning, lost in their own thoughts and memories. To help lift their spirits, he presented them with the rest of the gifts he had asked his mother to send him from India. For Mom, there was a hand-stitched pillow top. For Brad, a hand-tooled and dyed Indian wallet. For Dad, a small framed picture of a little Indian child with the inscription: *"Cause me to know the way wherein I walk,"* from Psalm 143:8.

Just then, Steve knocked on the door and entered. Raja looked from Steve to Mitsuko and wondered if either one of them had slept last night. You would have thought from the looks on their faces that they had lost their best friend.

With a sudden, sharp pang, he realized that perhaps that was exactly what they were thinking.

Raja excused himself from the table and joined Steve outside.

"Sorry I can't make it to the airport," Steve said. "But I wanted you to have this." It was a small, framed photograph of the two of them riding double on Steve's bike. Both of them were grinning. Underneath the photo, Steve had written *"There is a friend who sticks closer than a brother" (Proverbs 18:24).*

Raja reached into the pocket of his jacket and

handed Steve his red tie and red belt. He found it impossible to say anything and so he just hugged Steve for a long time. As Steve rode away on his bicycle, he called back, "Hey, Raja, I think Uganda is closer to India than America! Don't forget that, OK?"

As the family loaded his suitcases and drove to the airport, Raja was struck by the thought that he was doing everything in reverse. Could it have been nine months ago that he had stumbled down that airport ramp with shaky knees, marveling at the tall buildings and brilliant lights of the city? In the back seat of the station wagon, he sat sandwiched between Brad and Mitsuko as before. And while he hoped that Mitsuko would someday come to India, he knew with certainty that he would never ride with the Jade family again.

With the luggage checked in, they stood in the same waiting area as before. He remembered Mitsuko's sign waving back and forth above the crowd.

His flight was announced and the boarding began. While the first-class passengers filed past the checkpoint, Raja he turned to his host family for a final good-bye.

Shaking hands with Dad and Brad, he said, "Thank you for the many ways that you helped me while I was here in America."

Then he turned and hugged Mom. "Thanks Mom, for making me feel so much at home. I'll miss you very much."

Brad, Mom and Dad stepped back to allow Raja and

Mitsuko a final few moments of privacy.

Although she had been in so many ways the strong one, now Mitsuko could not keep the tears from streaming down her face. Raja wiped them with a gentle hand.

"Please don't cry, Mitsuko. In my Hindi Bible this morning, I read about faith, hope and love. And I knew that God had picked out that passage for us. I want you to read it and think about it today, OK? You and me, we share faith in the same God, we have hope for our future together, and we have love blessing us in so many ways—ways we cannot even begin to imagine. You think about that, promise?"

She nodded bravely but still could not speak. Instead, she pressed something into his palm, then kissed him on the cheek and ran to where her parents and brother were waiting. "Alvida!" they called to him, the Indian word for "good-bye."

"Last call for flight #649!" the announcement crackled from the speaker. Raja waved one last time and turned to walk up the ramp. As the plane lifted from the runway a few minutes later, he squeezed the gold locket and chain in his hand, then opened it. Inside was a tiny picture of Mitsuko and him. Steve must have taken it when they weren't paying attention. In the golden light of the dining room, their heads were bent together over homework.

"But the greatest of these is love" (1 Corinthians 13:13).

The End